Learning Grammar

with One Breath English

一口氣背文法

劉 毅 主編 / Laura E. Stewart 校閱

「一口氣英語」的目標，
是擊敗「啞巴英語」。

「一口氣背文法」既學會話，又學文法。

熟背全書216個句子，
就學會了216條文法規則。

背會話，學文法，不亦樂乎！

　　很多人從小學英文，讀到博士畢業，還是不會說，證明傳統學英文的方法完全失敗。我經過四十多年努力，發現背短句是學英文最好的方法，長句沒有人背得下來。小孩學語言都是從短句開始。

　　新來的 Beth Letcher 老師說，我的英文怎麼都是成語。我在大連學爾優國際教育趙艷花校長那裡，遇見一位王麗華校長，幾乎每一句話都用到中文成語，聽她講話令人佩服，Knowledge is power.。我看到 Beth，我和她說：*You are one in a million.*（妳是萬中選一。）*You are a needle in a haystack.*（妳是難得的人才。）我看她很忙，我就說：*You are as busy as a bear in a beehive.*（妳非常忙碌。）我們既然要學說英文，就要說好的句子，這些精彩的句子在「一口氣背呼口號英語」中都有。我看到一些年輕人，從美國回來，喜歡秀英文，我就跟他們說：*Shoot the moon.*（要達成不可能的任務。）*Step up to the plate.*（要開始行動。）*Swing for the fences.*（奮力一搏。）他們一聽到我說這些話，都會說 Shoot the moon?，我就知道他們聽不懂了。我說得有信心，是因爲我背過。

　　學生最感到爲難的是，背了「一口氣英語」，會說英文、會用英文演講，但是文法題目還是不會做。文法規則無限多，永遠學不完。我在 30 幾歲的時候，瘋狂研究文法，敎文法，背得滾瓜爛熟，編成了 700 多頁的「文法寶典」，所有難的文法題，都收入「文法寶典」，非常受讀者喜愛，因爲所有文法難題，書中都查得到。文法就是把句子歸納成規則，很多人以爲會文法就會造句，其實錯誤率有百分之五十以上。你讀了有限的規則，卻漏掉了無限多的例外，例如：過去式不一定表過去，有時還可以表現在，像 *I got a problem.*（我有一個問題。），不能説 *I get a problem.*（誤），那怎麼辦呢？

「一口氣背文法」每一回九句話代表九個文法規則，這九句話每一句都可以用在日常生活中，例如你背：I **get up** early every day.（我每天早起。）I **understand** this rule now.（我現在了解這條規則了。）Actions **speak** louder than words.（行動勝於言辭。）這三句話代表三個現在式的規則：第一句表現在的習慣，第二句表現在的動作，第三句表示不變的真理或諺語，用現在式動詞，但也有一些例外，懂得諺語用現在式，知道哪些諺語例外，有助於記憶。

麥可•傑克森在台上說：*I love you. I love you from the bottom of my heart. I really do.* 這三句話多麼容易學。在「一口氣背文法」中，就是以三句為一組，九句為一回，例如「句尾附加句」，你和朋友有爭執，你就可以說：*You don't want to do it, and neither do I.*（你不想做，我也不想做。）*Let's talk, shall we?*（我們談一談，好嗎？）*Let's not fight, all right?*（我們不要吵架，好嗎？）背了這三句話，說出來美國人會很震驚，因為一般中國人不會用句尾附加句。

在 Unit 17「倒裝、插入、省略」單元中，你天天都可以說：*What a beautiful day!*（多麼好的天氣！）*Never have I seen such a nice view.*（我從來沒看過這麼好的景色。）*I seldom, if ever, saw such a fine sight.*（即使有的話，我也很少看過這麼好的景色。）這三句話涵蓋了省略、倒裝、插入，你看，多麼精彩！

英文這個語言，大多可以歸納成文法規則。很多人一生鑽研文法，但是忘了「口說英語」。根據我的經驗，英文一定要使用，才會記得。這本書雖然是文法書，卻也是一本會話書。背完所有書中的句子，學會了文法規則，可以舉一反三。

劉 毅

CONTENTS

UNIT *1*

現在簡單式的用法

• •

　　這一回九句話，全部是「現在簡單式」的用法，現在式可表「現在的習慣」、「現在的動作」、「不變的真理」，甚至表「未來」等。背完這九句話，你就了解現在式的主要用法。

　　你是主角，和外國人在一起，談到你要出國旅遊，這九句話你天天都可以用到。

用手機掃瞄聽錄音

1. 現在簡單式的用法

I *get up* early every day.　　我每天早起。

I *understand* this rule now.　　我現在了解這條規定了。

Actions *speak* louder than
words.　　行動勝於言辭。

【二、三句強調實踐早起】

I *leave for* New York on
Sunday.　　我星期天要去紐約。

Let's get together when I
return.　　等我回來，我們再聚一聚。

I hope you *join* us.　　我希望你加入我們。

【二、三句強調邀請】

Call me if you have time.　　如你有空，打電話給我。

Do contact me if something
comes up.　　如果有事情發生，一定要連絡我。

The newspaper *says* the
weather may turn bad.　　報上說，天氣可能會變壞。

【一、二句強調打電話聯絡】

【文法解析】

1. I *get up* early every day.

   表「現在的習慣」，所以用現在式 get up。

2. I *understand* this rule now.

   表「現在的動作或狀態」，用現在式，其他如 I'm hungry.
   （我餓了。）

3. Actions *speak* louder than words.

   凡是不變的眞理或格言，用現在式。其他如：Lead *is* heavy.
   （鉛很重。）　　　 lead〔lɛd〕*n.* 鉛

   諺語不用現在式的例外有：

   Diamond *cut* diamond. (硬碰硬；勢均力敵。)【cut 是過去式】
   Care *killed* the cat. (憂慮傷身。)
   Curiosity *killed* the cat. (好奇傷身。)
   Accidents *will* happen. (天有不測風雲。)
   Faint heart never *won* fair lady.
   　　（唯英雄才能贏得美人；懦弱者永遠得不到美人。）

4. I *leave for* New York on Sunday.

   來去動詞 *come, go, start, leave* 等，可用現在式代替未來式。
   leave for 可看成動詞片語，作「前往」解。【詳見「文法寶典」p.327】

   【比較】*I leave for New York on Sunday.* 【常用】
   　　　　I'm leaving for New York on Sunday. 【常用】
   　　　　I will leave for New York on Sunday. 【少用】
   　　　　所謂少用就是不要用，因爲美國人聽起來不順，
   　　　　雖然文法正確，但不是他們平常所說的話。

UNIT 1~4

5. Let's get together *when I return*.

　　表時間或條件的副詞子句，要用現在式代替未來式。

6. I hope you *join* us.

　　凡是名詞子句做 *hope*、*assume*、*suppose* 等動詞的受詞時，
　　可用現在式代替未來式。

　　【比較】 *I hope you join us.*【常用】
　　　　　　 I hope you will join us.【少用】
　　　　　　 美國人常說：*I hope you like it.*【常用】，你如果說
　　　　　　 I hope you will like it.【少用】，沒有錯，但不合乎
　　　　　　 他們的習慣用法。【詳見「文法寶典」p.328】

7. *Call* me *if you have time*.　　命令句用原形動詞。

8. *Do contact* me *if something comes up*.

　　現在式動詞前加 do，表加強語氣。
　　come up 出現；發生（= *happen*）

9. The newspaper *says* the weather may turn bad.

　　凡是報紙上說或書上說，用現在式動詞。
　　turn bad 變壞（= *become bad*）
　　又如：The book *says* that women can live longer than
　　men.（這本書說，女人比男人長壽。）【詳見「文法寶典」p.329】
　　says 的發音唸成〔sɛz〕，say 唸成〔se〕，said 唸成〔sɛd〕，
　　saying 唸成〔'seɪŋ〕。

TEST *1* 時態

選出一個<u>最正確</u>的答案。

(　) 1. My father ＿＿＿＿＿ in his office every day.
(A) works 　　　 (B) work
(C) worked 　　 (D) working

(　) 2. The moon ＿＿＿＿＿ around the earth.
(A) move (B) moves (C) moving (D) moved

(　) 3. They ＿＿＿＿＿ a small house now.
(A) have (B) having (C) are 　　 (D) do

(　) 4. The cuckoo always ＿＿＿＿＿ its eggs in another bird's nest.
(A) lay 　 (B) lain 　 (C) lies 　 (D) lays

(　) 5. He will come back when his vacation ＿＿＿＿＿ over.
(A) is 　 (B) was 　 (C) will be (D) has been

(　) 6. The preparation of TV dinners ＿＿＿＿＿ only a few seconds.
(A) take 　 (B) takes 　 (C) taking 　 (D) are taken

(　) 7. ＿＿＿＿＿ these sheep yours?
(A) Are 　 (B) Is 　　 (C) Be 　　 (D) Was

( ) 8. My sister _____ a new watch the other day.
    (A) will buy   (B) bought
    (C) buys   (D) has bought

( ) 9. My father _____ me to the zoo if I pass the examination.
    (A) took   (B) will take
    (C) would take   (D) takes

( ) 10. Your plane _____ in ten minutes.
    (A) left   (B) will leave
    (C) leaves   (D) can leave

( ) 11. If the weather _____ nice tomorrow, I'll go on a picnic.
    (A) will be   (B) shall be
    (C) is going to be   (D) is

( ) 12. We do hope you _____ your stay with us.
    (A) enjoying   (B) should enjoy
    (C) are enjoyed   (D) enjoy

( ) 13. There _____ many people on the train when he got on.
    (A) was   (B) had
    (C) were   (D) have been

( ) 14. The girl fell off her bicycle yesterday and was
badly _____.
(A) hurt (B) hurts (C) hurting (D) hurted

( ) 15. _____ John and Mary absent yesterday?
(A) Was (B) Were (C) Had (D) Is

【Answers】

1. **A** every day「每天」，和現在式連用，現在式第三人稱單數，
動詞要加 s。

2. **B** 現在式表不變的真理。

3. **A** have「有」，表狀態，無進行式。

4. **D** cuckoo〔ˋkuku〕*n.* 布穀鳥
布穀鳥總是把蛋下在其他鳥巢裡。
現在式表習慣，過去如此，現在如此，未來也如此。
lay-laid-laid-laying「下（蛋）；產（卵）」，和 say-said-
said-saying 變化相同。
【比較】lie-lay-lain-lying「躺」

5. **A** 表「時間」的副詞子句，要用現在式代替未來式。

He will come back ***when*** *his vacation* ***is*** *over.*

6. **B** 表不變的事實用現在式。
準備電視晚餐只需幾秒鐘。

7. **A** 現在式表現在狀態，主詞 these sheep「這些羊」是複數，動詞用複數 Are。sheep「綿羊」單複數同型。

8. **B** *the other day*「幾天前」(= *a few days ago*)，和過去式連用。

9. **B** 根據句意，表「未來」。

10. **C** 你的飛機再過十分鐘就要起飛了。
來去動詞 leave 常用現在式代替未來式，<u>will leave 文法對，但極少用</u>。

11. **D** 表「條件」的副詞子句，要用現在式代替未來式。

If the weather is nice tomorrow, I'll go on a picnic.

12. **D** hope 後的名詞子句中，最常用現在式代替未來式，<u>will enjoy 文法對，但美國人極少用</u>。

13. **C** There *were* many people *on the train when he got on.*

當他上車的時候，火車上有很多人。

14. **A** 「受傷」要用 *be hurt* 或 *get hurt*。

15. **B** yesterday 和過去式連用，主詞 John and Mary 是複數，動詞用複數。

UNIT *2*

過去簡單式和未來式的用法

· ·

　　「過去簡單式」可表「過去的動作或狀態」，有時可代替「現在完成式」，或「過去完成式」，甚至「現在式」。「未來式」除了用 will 以外，還可用 *be going to* 表未來。背了這九句話，你就了解過去式和未來式的主要用法。

 你是主角，喜歡說英文，你一開口就是九句話，這些話你都常常用得到。

UNIT 1~4

2. 過去簡單式和未來式的用法

I *stayed up* late last night.

I *used to go* to bed early.

Did you *ever burn* the midnight oil?

【背誦技巧：昨晚熬夜、以前早睡】

我昨晚熬夜到很晚。

我以前習慣早睡。

你開過夜車嗎？

Mother *told* me it *was* harmful.

I never *did* this *before* I *went* to senior high.

I *did feel* uncomfortable.

【熬夜被媽媽罵；覺得不舒服】

媽媽告訴我這樣是有害的。

我上高中之前從未這麼做過。

我真的覺得不舒服。

I *gotta* go now.

I'*m going to see* a doctor.

I *will get* better soon.

【要走了，去看病】

我現在得走了。

我要去看醫生。

我很快就會好轉了。

【文法解析】

1. I *stayed up late last night.*

   表「過去的動作或狀態」，用過去簡單式。

   ⎧ *stay up*　熬夜
   ⎨ = sit up
   ⎩ = burn the midnight oil

2. I *used to go to bed early.*

   「*used to* + 原形動詞」，表「過去的習慣」，但現在沒有了，翻成「從前」，be used to + N/V-ing，表「習慣於」。

   【比較】① I *used to go* to bed early.—— 強調現在沒有早睡
   　　　　② I *am used to going* to bed early. (我習慣早睡。)
   　　　　③ I *was used to going* to bed early.
   　　　　　(我習慣了早睡。) —— 沒有強調現在的情形

3. *Did* you *ever burn* the midnight oil?

   過去式和 *ever*，*never* 連用，代替現在完成式，表「過去的經驗」。這句話等於 *Have* you *ever burned* the midnight oil?。burn the midnight oil 源自 *burn the midnight oil of the lamp* (現在不用)，字面意思是「半夜點油燈」，也就是「熬夜；開夜車」。

4. Mother *told* me it *was* harmful.

   當主要子句動詞是過去式 told，為配合時式一致，名詞子句動詞也用過去式。
   這句話也可說成：Mother told me it *would do* me harm.
   do sb. harm　對某人有害

5. I never *did* this *before I went to senior high.*

before 和 after 已經表明時間的先後，故可用過去式代替
過去完成式。這句話等於：I **had** never **done** this before
I went to senior high.

senior high 高中（= *senior high school*）
junior high 國中（= *junior high school*）

6. I *did feel* uncomfortable.

「did + 原形動詞」，表「加強語氣」。

這句話也可説成：I did feel uneasy.

uneasy〔ʌnˋizɪ〕*adj.* 不舒服的；不安的（= *not easy in body
or mind*）

7. I *gotta* go *now.*

gotta，唸成〔ˋɡɑtə〕，源自於 got to，作「必須」解，
表示現在。

I *gotta* go now.【詳見「文法寶典」p.350】
= I'*ve got to* go now.
= I *have to* go now.

8. I'*m going to see* a doctor.

「be going to + 原形動詞」表「未來打算做某事」。

9. I *will get* better *soon.*

現在的英文裡，未來式通常都用 will，少用 shall。這句
話也可説成：I will recover soon.（我很快就會恢復。）或
I will get well soon.（我很快就會好了。）

recover〔rɪˋkʌvɚ〕*v.* 恢復　　*get well* 復原；病癒

TEST *2* 時態

選出一個<u>最正確</u>的答案。

(　) 1. Tom ＿＿＿＿＿ up early this morning.
(A) to get　(B) get　　(C) gets　(D) got

(　) 2. She put on her hat and ＿＿＿＿＿ out.
(A) go　　(B) goes　(C) went　(D) to go

(　) 3. They ＿＿＿＿＿ too much coffee last night.
(A) drank　(B) drink　　(C) drunk　(D) drinking

(　) 4. The man hit by a car ＿＿＿＿＿ the next day.
(A) dies　　(B) will die　(C) died　　(D) by dying

(　) 5. You ＿＿＿＿＿ see a doctor now.
(A) have got　　　　　(B) gotta
(C) get to　　　　　　(D) get

(　) 6. I ＿＿＿＿＿ you one of these days.
(A) will see　　　　　(B) have seen
(C) had seen　　　　　(D) saw

(　) 7. It ＿＿＿＿＿ here last night.
(A) not rain　　　　　(B) did not rain
(C) was not rain　　　(D) do not rain

(　) 8. He ＿＿＿＿＿ to school two hours ago.
(A) went　　　　　　　(B) go
(C) have gone　　　　　(D) has gone

( ) 9. She _____ such a beautiful song before.
(A) never heard (B) ever heard
(C) hears (D) didn't hear

( ) 10. Mr. Black _____ a new shirt last week.
(A) buys (B) brought
(C) bought (D) is buying

( ) 11. He _____ the newspaper last night.
(A) reads (B) read
(C) don't read (D) wasn't read

( ) 12. The map isn't on the wall now, but it _____ before.
(A) is (B) was (C) are (D) were

( ) 13. I called you at six yesterday evening, but you _____ home.
(A) aren't (B) are (C) weren't (D) couldn't

( ) 14. After a long walk, John and I _____ both tired.
(A) is (B) am (C) was (D) were

( ) 15. One of the students in John's class _____ sick yesterday.
(A) were (B) had (C) did (D) was

【Answers】

1. **D** this morning「今天早上」和過去式連用。

2. **C** 前面 put 是過去式。 她戴上帽子走出去。

3. **A** last night「昨晚」和過去式連用。
drink–drank–drunk「喝」。

4. **C** The man *hit by a car **died** the next day.
the next day 隔天

5. **B** You ***gotta*** see a doctor now.
= You'***ve got to*** see a doctor now.
= You ***have to*** see a doctor now.

6. **A** ┌ ***one of these days*** 不久會有一天【表未來】
│ = some of these days
└ = some day
┌ = sometime soon
└ = sooner or later

7. **B** 同第3題。主詞 It 指「天氣」。

8. **A** two hours ago 和過去式連用。

9. **A** never heard 等於 has never heard。過去式和 never 連用，
代替現在完成式。【詳見「文法寶典」p.330, p.335】

10. **C** buy–bought–bought「買」，bring–brought–brought「帶來」。

11. **B** read「讀」三態變化相同，在此為過去式。

12. **B** 地圖現在不在牆上，但是以前在。
… it ***was*** (*on the wall*) ***before***.

13. **C** 根據句意，前句是過去式，後句也用過去式。

14. **D** 根據句意用過去式，主詞 John and I 是複數，動詞用複數。

15. **D** One *of the students in John's class* ***was*** sick yesterday.

約翰班上的一位學生昨天生病了。

UNIT *3*

現在完成式、現在完成進行式、過去完成式的用法

「現在完成式」可表示「剛剛完成的動作」、「過去到現在的經驗」;「現在完成進行式」強調持續的動作;過去的過去用「過去完成式」。背了這九個句子,你才會用「現在完成式」、「現在完成進行式」和「過去完成式」。說話的時候用文法造句,很容易出錯,背的句子說起來最有信心。

 這一回你和外國朋友談到你生病的情形。你是主角,喜歡說英文。

3. 現在完成式、現在完成進行式、 過去完成式的用法

I *have* just *taken* medicine.	我剛吃了藥。
I *have* never *been* so ill before.	我以前從來沒有病得那麼重。
I *haven't eaten* anything today.	我今天還沒吃東西。

【背誦技巧：吃藥→感嘆病重→沒吃東西】

Five days *have passed* since I got sick.	自從我生病已經五天了。
I *have sent* two emails this morning.	我今天早上已經寄了二封電子郵件。
I *have been waiting* for my friends.	我一直在等我的朋友。

【生病五天→寂寞發 email→等朋友來看】

I recovered sooner than I *had expected*.	我復原比我預期得快。
I *had hoped* to go to my friend's party.	我原本希望去參加朋友的聚會。
No sooner *had* I *left* the house than it began to rain.	我一離開屋子就開始下雨。

【病好→感嘆沒參加聚會】這三句都是過去完成式。

【文法解析】

1. I *have just taken* medicine.

「現在完成式」可表剛剛完成的動作，常附有副詞，如：
just（剛剛），*now*（現在），*today*（今天），*already*（已經），
yet（尚（未）），*this week*（本週）等。這句話也可說成：
I just took medicine.
take medicine 吃藥，不能寫成 *eat medicine*（誤）。

2. I *have never been* so ill before.

「現在完成式」可表過去某時到現在的經驗，常附有副詞：
ever（曾經），*never*（從未），*before*（以前），*in one's life*
（在某人的一生中），*once*（曾經；一次），*twice*（兩次）等。
「過去簡單式」也可表經驗，詳見「文法寶典」p.330。

3. I *haven't eaten* anything *today*.

「現在完成式」可表示過去的動作，其結果影響到現在。
這句話的含意是 I'm hungry.（我很餓。）

4. Five days *have passed since I got sick*.

「現在完成式」可和 since 所引導的副詞子句連用，此時，
主要子句用現在完成式，*since* 子句用過去式。這句話等於：
It *has been* five days *since I got sick*.

5. I *have sent* two emails *this morning*.

「現在完成式」可和 *this morning*，*this afternoon*，*this
evening* 等副詞片語連用，依說話的時間來決定用「現在完
成式」或「過去式」。【詳見「文法寶典」p.335】

【比較】I *have sent* two emails this morning. (早上説)

I *sent* two emails this morning. (下午説)

（我今天早上寄了二封電子郵件。）

email〔ˋiˏmel〕*n.* 電子郵件（= *e-mail*）

6. I *have been waiting* for my friends.

「現在完成進行式」強調動作持續進行。

【比較】I *have waited* for my friends.【語氣較弱】

I *have been waiting* for my friends.【語氣較強】

【詳見「文法寶典」p.349】

7. I recovered sooner *than I had expected*.

過去先發生者用「過去完成式」，後發生者用「過去式」。

8. I *had hoped* to go to my friend's party.

hope（希望），*expect*（期待），*suppose*（以為），*intend*（打算）等的過去完成式，表示過去未實現的希望或計劃。

【詳見「文法寶典」p.339, 423】

9. *No sooner* had I *left* the house *than it began to rain*.

no sooner ~ than… 一～就…

no 在這個片語中是副詞，等於 not at all，字面意思是「一點都沒有比…早」，引申為「一～就…」。no sooner 和過去完成式連用，表動作先發生，than 後用過去式。

表示「一～就…」的連接詞很多，詳見「文法寶典」p.496。

這句話是倒裝句，可以説成：I *had no sooner left* the house *than* it began to rain.【倒裝句的用法，詳見「文法寶典」p.629】

TEST *3* 時態

選出一個<u>最正確</u>的答案。

(　　) 1. He has _____ to the United States; he isn't here now.
    (A) been   (B) been going
    (C) gone   (D) been gone

(　　) 2. The Browns _____ there for ten years.
    (A) is living   (B) has lived
    (C) have lived   (D) are living

(　　) 3. She _____ the movie three times already.
    (A) has seen   (B) sees
    (C) will see   (D) is seeing

(　　) 4. I _____ him this morning.
    (A) see   (B) will have seen
    (C) was seeing   (D) have seen

(　　) 5. I _____ to call on you.
    (A) have intended
    (B) will have intended
    (C) had intended
    (D) will intend

( ) 6. They are sure that he _____ in Hong Kong already.
  (A) arrives   (B) arrived
  (C) will arrive   (D) has arrived

( ) 7. He _____ seriously ill for the past few days.
  (A) is   (B) was
  (C) has been   (D) have been

( ) 8. Nancy's parents _____ any news from her yet.
  (A) received   (B) hasn't received
  (C) haven't received   (D) didn't receive

( ) 9. Most of the people over there _____ worked for more than ten hours.
  (A) are   (B) have
  (C) have been   (D) would have been

( ) 10. The baby has _____.
  (A) falling asleep   (B) fallen asleep
  (C) fell sleeping
  (D) been fallen sleeping

( ) 11. He _____ all afternoon. He is very tired.
  (A) works   (B) will work
  (C) has worked   (D) had worked

(　) 12. Mary ＿＿＿＿＿＿ just finished her homework when the mailman came.
  (A) has (B) will have (C) had (D) was

(　) 13. They ＿＿＿＿＿＿ when we arrived.
  (A) had left   (B) has left
  (C) were left   (D) leaves

(　) 14. After my father ＿＿＿＿＿＿ all his life, he decided to travel around the world.
  (A) works   (B) has worked
  (C) had worked (D) has been working

(　) 15. He ＿＿＿＿＿＿ down than he fell asleep.
  (A) had no sooner sat (B) sooner sat
  (C) sat no sooner (D) sat sooner

【Answers】

1. **C** *have gone to* 表「已經去～」，還沒回來；*have been to* 表「曾經去過」，已經回來。

2. **C** 「現在完成式」可表「完成＋繼續」。The Browns「布朗一家人」為複數，助動詞用 have。

3. **A** 「現在完成式」和次數連用。

4. **D** 「現在完成式」和 this morning 連用，表示剛完成的動作，說話者在早上說這句話。如在下午，則說：I saw him this morning.【參照 p.21 第 5 句】

5. **C** *I had intended to*…表示「我本來打算…」。【參照 p.22 第 8 句】
   call on sb. 拜訪某人

6. **D** 「現在完成式」和 already 連用。

7. **C** for the past few days「過去幾天」，和「現在完成式」連用。

8. **C** *not…yet*「尚未」，和「現在完成式」連用。

9. **B** 主詞是 Most，動詞看所代替的名詞而定。

   Most *of the people over there* **have worked** *for more*

   than ten hours.

10. **B** *fall asleep*「睡著」；fall 的三態變化：fall–fell–fallen。

    The baby has fallen asleep.
    = The baby has gone to sleep. 【正，表動作完成】
    The baby has slept.【誤】
    The baby has slept for two hours.【正，表動作持續】

11. **C** all afternoon「整個下午」，和完成式連用。

12. **C** 兩個過去的動作，先發生的用「**過去完成式**」，後發生的用「**過去式**」。

13. **A** 同第 12 題。

    They had left **when we arrived**.
    　　先發生　　　　　　後發生

14. **C** 過去的過去用「**過去完成式**」。

15. **A** 他一坐下就睡著了。
    no sooner 和過去完成式連用。【詳見「文法寶典」p.497】

UNIT 4

現在進行式、過去進行式、
未來進行式的用法

● ●

現在進行式通常表示「現在正在進行的動作」，有時表「未來」，有些動詞沒有進行式。過去進行式表示「過去某時正在進行的動作」。未來進行式表示「未來某時正在進行的動作」。「過去進行式」和「未來進行式」的句子，不背誰會說？

 這一回你是主角，和外國朋友談到你要去紐約。

1. I'm leaving. Have a safe trip.

2. It's raining cats and dogs. It sure is.

3. My mother is always complaining. What about?

4. 現在進行式、過去進行式、未來進行式的用法

I'*m leaving*. 　　　　　　　　　我要走了。

It'*s raining* cats and dogs. 　　　雨下得很大。

My mother *is* always 　　　　　　我媽媽老是在抱怨。
　complaining.

【背誦技巧：要走了，下雨，媽媽
　又抱怨】

I'*m going* away for a week. 　　　我計劃出去一個禮拜。

It'*s getting* colder. 　　　　　　天氣越來越冷了。

I *prefer* warm days. 　　　　　　我比較喜歡溫暖的天氣。

【媽媽抱怨→出去一星期→天氣冷】

I *was packing* when Mom 　　　　當媽媽回家時我正在打
　got home. 　　　　　　　　　　　包。

I *promised* her I would stay 　　　我答應她我會小心安全。
　safe.

I *will be enjoying* my trip 　　　明天的此時我將正在享受
　at this time tomorrow. 　　　　　我的旅行。

【媽媽看到我打包→我保證安全】

英文依動詞的變化有 12 種時態：

現在
過去
未來

$\times$

簡單式
完成式
進行式
完成進行式

= 12 種時態

以動詞 write 為例：

	簡單式	完成式	進行式	完成進行式
現在	write	have written	are writing	have been writing
過去	wrote	had written	were writing	had been writing
未來	will write	will have written	will be writing	will have been writing

　　最常用的時態是：**現在、過去、未來**，第二常用的是：**現在進行、現在完成**，第三常用的是：**過去進行、過去完成**，我們沒有講到的未來完成式、過去完成進行式、未來完成進行式，美國人在口語中使用機會太少，文章中很少出現。

UNIT 1~4

【文法解析】

1. I'*m leaving*.

「來去動詞」常用現在進行式，表示不久的未來。

「來去動詞」有：*go, come, start, leave, return, arrive* 等。

【詳見「文法寶典」p.341】

2. It'*s raining cats and dogs*.

表示現在正在進行的動作，用「現在進行式」。

rain cats and dogs (下傾盆大雨) 是慣用語，不可寫成 *rain dogs and cats* (誤)。背的時候，記住 c 在前，d 在後，就不會錯了，這個片語也可説成 rain heavily 或 rain hard。

3. My mother *is always complaining*.

現在進行式和 *always* (老是)，*continually* (常常)，*constantly* (老是)，*forever* (= *for ever*) (老是)，*all the time* (一直)，*all the while* (一直) 等表「連續」的時間副詞連用時，通常表示説話者認爲不良的習慣或不耐煩。

complain〔kəm'plen〕*v.* 抱怨

4. I'*m going away for a week*.

現在進行式可表示「現在的安排」或「計劃未來要做的事」。

go away 的意思是「離開」或「(爲度假而) 離家」，和 go out 「(短時間) 出門」不一樣。

【比較】

I'm going out for a week. (誤)

I'm going out for $\left\{ \begin{array}{l} \text{a while.} \\ \text{an hour.} \\ \text{a few hours.} \end{array} \right.$ (我要出去 $\left\{ \begin{array}{l} \text{一會兒。} \\ \text{一小時。} \\ \text{幾小時。} \end{array} \right.$)

5. It'*s getting* colder.

   get, become, run, go 等的進行式，表示「越來越」。這句話
   也可説成：It's getting cold. (天氣越來越冷了。)

6. I *prefer* warm days.

   有無限多的動詞沒有進行式，像表「**事實狀態**」的動詞，
   如 be, have, belong，或「**心理狀態**」，如 love, hate,
   dislike, foget 等。【詳見「文法寶典」p.343, 344 】
   prefer〔prɪˋfɝ〕*v.* 比較喜歡

7. I *was packing* **when** Mom got home.

   「過去進行式」表過去某時正在進行的動作。
   pack〔pæk〕*v.* 打包　*n.* 一包；小包

8. I *promised* her I would stay safe.

   表一時性的動詞沒有進行式，動作開始就是結束，沒有進
   行的可能，如 ***promise*** (答應)，***accept*** (接受)，***allow*** (允
   許)，***admit*** (承認) 等。【詳見「文法寶典」p.344 】
   stay safe 小心安全 (= *be careful*)

9. I *will be enjoying* my trip *at this time tomorrow.*

   「未來進行式」表未來某時正在進行的動作。

UNIT 1 ~ 4

TEST *4* 時態

選出一個<u>最正確</u>的答案。

( ) 1. He _____ fault with me.
  (A) forever finds (B) forever found
  (C) will forever find (D) is forever finding

( ) 2. We _____ married in March.
  (A) are getting (B) get
  (C) are (D) were getting

( ) 3. I _____ you are right.
  (A) thought (B) am thinking
  (C) have thought (D) think

( ) 4. What _____ about now?
  (A) you think (B) you are thinking
  (C) are you think (D) are you thinking

( ) 5. He told me that she _____ in the kitchen.
  (A) is cooking (B) was cooking
  (C) has cooked (D) has been cooking

( ) 6. He _____ that he is wrong.
  (A) admits (B) admitted
  (C) is admitting (D) was admitting

( ) 7. Look! The sun _____.
  (A) risen (B) rises
  (C) rose now (D) is rising

( ) 8. _____ Mr. Brown working in the garden?
    (A) Does   (B) Has   (C) Is   (D) Will

( ) 9. The dog _____ on the floor now.
    (A) lying   (B) was lying
    (C) is lying   (D) has lying

( ) 10. I _____ TV at 8 o'clock last night.
    (A) will watch   (B) was watching
    (C) would like to watch
    (D) had watched

( ) 11. While we were _____ dinner, the mailman
    came.
    (A) eating   (B) eat   (C) ate   (D) eaten

( ) 12. What _____ when the telephone rang?
    (A) are you doing   (B) have you done
    (C) were you doing
    (D) have you been doing

( ) 13. Her sister _____ at that time.
    (A) is dancing   (B) has danced
    (C) was dancing   (D) has been dancing

( ) 14. He _____ Chinese for five years before he
    came to Taiwan.
    (A) was studying   (B) has studies
    (C) had been studying
    (D) has been studying

UNIT 1~4

(　) 15. We _____ English for two and a half years.
　　　　(A) are studying　　　(B) have been studying
　　　　(C) have been studied　(D) have studying

【Answers】

1. **D**　他不斷地挑我的錯。

　　「現在進行式」和表「連續」的副詞連用，如 always，forever，表示說話者現在認爲不良的習慣。【詳見「文法寶典」p.342】　***find fault with*** 挑錯；挑剔

2. **A**　我們將在三月結婚。

　　「現在進行式」可表現在的安排或計劃未來要做的事。

3. **D**　think 爲表「心理情感狀態」的動詞，沒有進行式。

4. **D**　think 在此作「想」解，有進行式。

5. **B**　爲配合主要子句中的過去式，名詞子句用過去進行式。

6. **A**　admit「承認」爲一時性動詞，沒有進行式。

7. **D**　表現在正在進行。　　8. **C**　同上。

9. **C**　lie–lay–lain–lying「躺」，now 和現在進行式連用。

10. **B**　表過去某時正在進行。

11. **A**　同上。

While *we **were eating** dinner*, the mailman came.

12. **C**　同上。　　13. **C**　同上。

14. **C**　「過去完成式」可用「過去完成進行式」加強持續的語氣。

15. **B**　「現在完成式」可用「現在完成進行式」加強持續的語氣。

UNIT 5

被動語態（Passive Voice）

• •

語態有「主動語態」和「被動語態」。大原則是，及物動詞「人」做主詞用「主動」，「非人」做主詞用「被動」。不及物動詞沒有受詞，所以沒有被動。有太多例外，所以，背句子是最簡單的方法。

 你是主角，說話說個不停。

5. 被動語態（Passive Voice）

The World Trade Center *was destroyed*.	世貿中心被摧毀了。
The Freedom Tower *has been constructed*.	自由塔已經興建。
I have *become acquainted with* many people.	我認識了許多人。

【一、二句意思相連】

I *feel* so *excited*.	我覺得非常興奮。
I *had* my clothes *pressed*.	我拿我的衣服去燙。
This shirt will *wear* for a long time.	這件襯衫很耐穿。

【認識很多人，興奮；二、三句談到 衣服】

The brand *is selling* well.	這個牌子賣得很好。
My friend is about to *marry*.	我的朋友要結婚了。
I'*m delighted* at the news.	聽到這個消息我很高興。

【二、三句意思相關】

【文法解析】

1. The World Trade Center *was destroyed*.

   語態分成「主動語態」和「被動語態」二種，原則上，及物動詞非人做主詞要用被動，這句話可加長爲：The World Trade Center was destroyed on September ll, 2001.
   destroy〔dɪ'strɔɪ〕*v.* 破壞；摧毀

2. The Freedom Tower *has been constructed*.

   這句話是「現在完成式被動」，被動式是「be + p.p.」，現在完成式被動是「have been + p.p.」，主詞是第三人稱單數，所以用 has。　　construct〔kən'strʌkt〕*v.* 建造

3. I have *become acquainted with* many people.

   ***become*, *get*, *grow* + 過去分詞，表轉變。**
   　　be acquainted with 認識（= *know*）
   　　become acquainted with 認識
   　　= *become familiar with*
   　　= *get to know*

4. I *feel* so *excited*.

   be 動詞可用 *feel*, *lie*, *stand*, *remain* 等動詞代替。He ***remained unmarried***. （他還沒結婚。）【詳見「文法寶典」p.387】
   「情感動詞」被動表示主動意思，如：excite（使興奮）、disappoint（使失望）、interest（使感興趣）、delight（使高興）等。【詳見「文法寶典」p.389】

5. I *had* my clothes *pressed*.

   「have, get + 受詞 + 過去分詞」表示自己不做，而讓他人做。【詳見「文法寶典」p.387】　　press〔prɛs〕*v.* 熨燙

6. This shirt will *wear* for a long time.

下面動詞可**用主動代替被動**：*wear*（穿；耐用），*catch*（抓住），*sell*（賣），*read*（讀），*cut*（切），*carry*（攜帶），*flood*（淹沒），*peel*（剝皮）。例如：The novel reads well.（這本小說讀起來很有趣。）【詳見「文法寶典」p.388】

7. The brand *is selling* well.

有些進行式動詞，主動代替被動。【詳見「文法寶典」p.388】
brand〔brænd〕*n.* 品牌
這句話也可說成：The brand sells well. 主動進行代替被動進行的情況不多，就把這句話當作慣用語來背。不可說成：*The brand is sold well.*（誤）

8. My friend is about to *marry.*

有些動詞**主動和被動意義相同**，如 *marry*（結婚），*rent*（出租），determine（決定），graduate（畢業），starve（飢餓），derive（起源），prepare（準備）等。【詳見「文法寶典」p.389】

My friend is about to $\left\{\begin{array}{l} \textit{marry.} 【主動】 \\ \textit{get married.} \\ \textit{be married.} \end{array}\right.$【被動】
【這三句話意義相同】

「和～結婚」須用 be married to，不可用 *be married with*（誤）。
be about to + *V.* 將要；正要

9. I'*m delighted* at the news.

情感動詞以人做主詞，用過去分詞，不表被動。
delight〔dɪ'laɪt〕*v.* 使高興
這句話可說成：The news delighted me. 改成被動後，介詞可用 at, by, with。

I'*m delighted* $\left\{\begin{array}{l} \textit{at} \\ \textit{by} \\ \textit{with} \end{array}\right\}$ the news.

TEST *5* 被動語態

選出一個<u>最正確</u>的答案。

( ) 1. The dog _____ in the park.
    (A) found   (B) has found
    (C) being found   (D) was found

( ) 2. He _____ about his sickness.
    (A) upset   (B) upsets
    (C) is upset   (D) is upsetting

( ) 3. When she appeared, I _____.
    (A) was astonished   (B) feel astonished
    (C) am astonished   (D) was astonishing

( ) 4. What is done _____ done and regret is of no use.
    (A) is   (B) can't   (C) are   (D) has

( ) 5. Some of his money _____ on books.
    (A) are spent   (B) will spend
    (C) has spent   (D) is spent

( ) 6. I think the library is _____ today.
    (A) opened   (B) closed   (C) close   (D) to closing

( ) 7. All his homework _____ already.
    (A) are finished   (B) has finished
    (C) will be finished   (D) has been finished

(   ) 8. Everything near the North Pole _____ ice and snow almost all the year round.
      (A) is covered with   (B) covered with
      (C) is covered on   (D) covered on

(   ) 9. This book will get you _____ with many kinds of flowers.
      (A) acquainted   (B) acquainting
      (C) to acquaint   (D) be acquainted

(   ) 10. The house _____ to Mr. Brown last year.
      (A) was sold   (B) is sold
      (C) has sold   (D) sold

(   ) 11. Don't count your chickens before they _____.
      (A) will hatch   (B) had hatched
      (C) are hatched   (D) were hatched

(   ) 12. The letter is _____ in Chinese.
      (A) write   (B) wrote   (C) writing   (D) written

(   ) 13. I can't find the cat anywhere; I think it _____.
      (A) is losing   (B) is lost
      (C) has lost   (D) was lost

(   ) 14. Mary was seen _____ English.
      (A) study   (B) being studied
      (C) to studying   (D) studying

(　) 15. English is ＿＿＿＿ in every school.
　　　　(A) teach　　　　　(B) teaching
　　　　(C) taught　　　　　(D) teacher

【Answers】

1. **D**　原則上，及物動詞「非人」做主詞用被動。

2. **C**　upset〔ʌpˋsɛt〕v. 使生氣；使煩惱，是情感動詞，和
　　excite（使興奮）、interest（使感興趣）一樣，修飾人
　　要用被動，但無被動意義。

> It upset me.（它使我煩惱。）
> ＝ I was upset.（我很煩惱。）
> ＝ It was upsetting to me.（它令我煩惱。）

3. **A**　astonish〔əˋstɑnɪʃ〕v. 使吃驚，是情感動詞。

4. **A**　What is done 是名詞子句，為單數，be 動詞用 is，根
　　據句意用被動，這句話的意思是「做了就做了，後悔沒
　　有用。」　regret〔rɪˋgrɛt〕n. 後悔
　　of no use 沒有用的（＝ *useless*）

5. **D**　主動：He spends some of his money on books.
　　Some of his money 當主詞，動詞用單數。

6. **B**　中文：圖書館關閉。
　　英文：The library is closed.【正】
　　　　　The library is close.【誤，這句話的意思是「圖書館
　　　　　很近。」】

中文：圖書館開放了。

英文：The library is open.【正】

The library is opened.【誤】

open 和 close 容易搞混，背句子最安全。

7. D　現在完成式的被動是：have been + p.p.。

8. A　*be covered with*　被～覆蓋【詳見「文法寶典」p.391】

the North Pole 北極　　*all the year round* 一年到頭

9. A　*be acquainted with* 熟悉【詳見「文法寶典」p.391】

get you (*to be*) acquainted with 中的 to be 必須省略。

10. A　這間房子去年被賣給布朗先生。

11. C　【諺】不要打如意算盤。

count〔kaʊnt〕*v.* 數　　hatch〔hætʃ〕*v.* 孵化

這句話字面的意思是「在小雞還沒孵化之前不要數會有幾隻雞。」

12. D　這封信是用中文寫的。

13. B　The cat *is lost*. (貓不見了。)

= The cat *is missing*.

14. D　感官動詞的被動，後面可用 to + 原形或 V-ing。

本題表「無意中看到或聽到」，應用 V-ing，不可用 to + 原形。

We saw Mary studying English.

= Mary was seen studying English.

15. C　teach「教」的三態變化：teach–taught–taught。

UNIT *6*

助動詞（Auxiliary Verbs）

• •

　　這一回九句話你背完後，就知道助動詞的用法了。可用這些句子來邀請你的朋友，搭捷運（MRT）去暢貨中心（outlet mall）。

 你是主角，喜歡說英文，看到外國人，就說個不停。

1.
Would you tell me where to go?
Sure.

2. Shall I take you to the outlet mall?
OK.

3. You may well be surprised.
We'll see.

6. 助動詞（Auxiliary Verbs）

UNIT 5~8

Would you tell me where to go?

你能告訴我去哪裡嗎？

Shall I take you to the outlet mall?

要我帶你去暢貨中心嗎？

You *may well* be surprised.

你可能會很驚訝。

【背誦技巧：Would you~？　Shall I~？】

I *will* shop for hours at a time.

我一次買東西總要花幾個小時。

The traffic *must* be heavy.

交通流量一定很大。

We *can never* be *too* careful.

我們要非常非常小心。

【二、三句意思相關】

I *would rather* take the MRT.

我寧願搭捷運。

Would that we got here sooner!

要是我們早點到這裡就好了！

I *should have followed* your suggestion.

我早該聽你的建議。

【一、二句都有 would】

【文法解析】

1. *Would* you tell me where to go?

   疑問句中的 would，表示謙恭的請求，比 will 客氣，事實上是省略了 if 子句的假設法，含有 *...if I were to ask you?* 的意思，表示自己不該問而問。【詳見「文法寶典」p.308】

2. *Shall* I take you to the outlet mall?

   shall 用於一、三人稱疑問句，表示徵求對方的意見，此時的 Shall 等於 *Do you want...to*，例如：Shall we go? 等於 *Do you want to go?*【詳見「文法寶典」p.310, 311】

   outlet (ˈaʊtˌlɛt) *n.* 出口；名牌暢貨中心
   mall (mɔl) *n.* 購物中心

3. You *may well* be surprised.

   may well 很有理由；大可 (= *have good reason to*)；
   　　很可能 (= *be likely to*)
   may well 就是 may 的加強語氣。

   may as well 最好 (= *had better*)
   We *may as well* stay here. (我們最好待在這裡。)

4. I *will* shop for hours at a time.

   will 可表習性或傾向。
   Boys *will* be boys. (孩子總是孩子。)
   Accidents *will* happen. (天有不測風雲。)
   shop (ʃɑp) *v.* 購物　　*at a time* 一次

5. The traffic *must* be heavy.

   must + 原形　表「對現在的推測」
   must + have p.p.　表「對過去的推測」
   must + be V-ing　表「對現在或現在正在的推測」
   【詳見「文法寶典」p.319】　　heavy (ˈhɛvɪ) *adj.* 大量的

6. We *can never* be *too* careful.

cannot~too…　再怎麼…也不為過

這句話字面意思是「我們再怎麼小心也不為過」，也就是「我們
要非常非常小心」，也可説成：We must be extremely careful.

I *cannot* admire your beauty *too* much.

（我怎麼讚美妳的美麗也不為過。）

7. I *would rather* take the MRT.

would rather (= *would sooner*) + 原形動詞，作「寧願」解。
這句話也可説成：I prefer to take the MRT. (我比較喜歡
搭捷運。)

MRT 捷運 (= *Mass Rapid Transit*)，原則上，專有名詞前
不加冠詞，但船、艦隊、鐵道名稱例外，要加 the。【詳見
「文法寶典」p.63】

8. *Would that* we got here sooner!

Would that (= *I wish* = *If only*) 作「但願」解。【詳見「文法
寶典」p.370】

Would that　⎫　I could be there tomorrow.
I wish　　 ⎬　（但願我明天能在那裡。）
If only　　⎭　I were there now. (但願我現在在那裡。)
　　　　　　　　I had been there yesterday.
　　　　　　　　（但願我昨天在那裡。）

9. I *should have followed* your suggestion.

should have p.p. 表「過去該做而未做」，為「與過去事實
相反」的假設法。

【比較】I should go. (我應該去。)【表現在或未來該去而未去】

　　　　I should have gone. (我早該去的。)【事實上未去】

should, would, could, might 為假設法助動詞。【詳見「文法寶
典」p.361】　　follow ('falo) *v.* 聽從

TEST *6* 助動詞

選出一個<u>最正確</u>的答案。

( ) 1. We cannot but _____.
    (A) laugh   (B) laughing
    (C) to laugh   (D) laughed

( ) 2. May you _____!
    (A) success   (B) successful
    (C) succeed   (D) successfully

( ) 3. I can't find my bag. It _____ stolen just now.
    (A) has   (B) must have been
    (C) will have been   (D) had

( ) 4. You ought _____ your homework last night.
    (A) do   (B) to do
    (C) did   (D) to have done

( ) 5. Which would you rather _____, go to the movies or stay at home?
    (A) do   (B) doing   (C) to do   (D) did

( ) 6. Would you like _____ for a walk?
    (A) to go   (B) going   (C) to going   (D) go

( ) 7. He _____ to go fishing in the river.
    (A) may   (B) might   (C) used   (D) would

(　　)　8. He is used to _____ late.
      (A) sleep   (B) sleeps
      (C) slept   (D) sleeping

(　　)　9. Mary likes the flowers and Jane _____.
      (A) does too   (B) likes too
      (C) is too   (D) is like to

(　　) 10. You _____ have to come home at once.
      (A) aren't (B) don't (C) can (D) must

(　　) 11. We know that a housewife does not need _____ for food every day.
      (A) going shoping
      (B) to go shoping
      (C) to going shopping
      (D) to go shopping

(　　) 12. A: May I pick this flower?
      B: No, you _____.
      (A) will not   (B) shall not
      (C) need not   (D) must not

(　　) 13. A: Must I go at once?
      B: No, you _____ not. You may stay.
      (A) must (B) need (C) will (D) may

UNIT 5~8

( ) 14. A: You must be here at six tomorrow morning.

   B: Sorry. I ＿＿＿＿ be here so early.

    (A) need (B) may (C) must (D) can't

( ) 15. You have good reason to rely on him.

   = You may ＿＿＿＿ rely on him.

    (A) very (B) well (C) full (D) as well

【Answers】

1. **A** ***cannot but*** + 原形 不得不【詳見「文法寶典」p.314, 419 助動詞的慣用語】

2. **C** 「May + 主詞 + 原形」表「祈願」。

3. **B** 「***must have*** + *p.p.*」表現在對過去的推測。

  just now 剛剛；現在【在此作「剛剛」解】

  我找不到我的袋子。一定是剛剛被偷了。

4. **D** 「***ought to have*** + *p.p.*」表「過去應該做而未做」，等於 should have + p.p.。

5. **A** ***would rather*** (= *would sooner*) + 原形，作「寧願」解。

  也可加長爲：would $\left\{ \begin{array}{l} \text{rather} \\ \text{sooner} \end{array} \right\}$ + 原形…than + 原形…

        (寧願…而不願…)

  【詳見「文法寶典」p.310】

6. **A** ***would like to*** + 原形　想要（= want to + 原形），和 like
「喜歡」不同。【詳見「文法寶典」p.310】

7. **C** 「***used to*** + 原形」表「從前」，暗示現在沒有了。

8. **D** ***be used to*** + ***V-ing*** 習慣於
他習慣晚起。　　***sleep late*** 晚起（= *get up late*）

9. **A** Jane ***does*** too = Jane likes the flowers too。
助動詞 do 可代替前面所說的話。

10. **B** ***don't have to*** 不必（= *don't need to*）

11. **D** 同上。(B) 應改成 to go ***shopping***。
我們知道，家庭主婦不必每天去買菜。

12. **D** 對於 "May I…?" 的回答，肯定的用 "Yes, you may."
否定的用 "No, you may not." 或 "No, you must not."
may not 不可以　　***must not*** 不准；不行
pick〔pɪk〕*v.* 採；摘

13. **B** 對於 "Must I…?" 的回答，肯定的用 "Yes, you must."
否定的用 "No, you need not." 【詳見「文法寶典」p.318】
need not 不必　　***at once*** 立刻

14. **D** ***can not*** 不行；不能；不可能

15. **B** 你大可依賴他。
may well + 原形　很有理由；大可以（= *have good reason to*）
may as well + 原形　最好（= *had better*）
rely on 依賴（= *depend on*）【詳見「文法寶典」p.317】

UNIT 7

不定詞（Infinitive）

　　這一回九句是在購物中心（the mall）所說的話，每一句都可以主動說，天天用得到。背完九句話以後，就能了解不定詞的主要用法。文法是一種歸納，讓你能舉一反三。原則上，不定詞片語可當名詞、形容詞，或副詞。

 你是活潑的主角，喜歡說英文。

UNIT 5~8

7. 不定詞（Infinitive）

To hang around here is great.

We've got a lot *to do*.

I'm impressed *to see* so many things.

【背誦技巧：三句都有不定詞】

在這裡逛很棒。

我們有很多事可做。

看到這麼多東西我真是大開眼界。

I *see* a few groups *performing* nearby.

To tell the truth, I don't have enough money.

I *intended to buy* a smartphone.

【二、三句意思相連】

我看到幾群人在附近表演。

老實說，我錢不夠。

我打算買一支智慧型手機。

Is it possible *for you to lend* me some money?

Would you be kind *enough to help* me?

I promise *to pay* you back soon.

【三句話都是借錢】

你可能借我一些錢嗎？

你可不可以好心一點幫幫我？

我保證很快還給你。

【文法解析】

1. *To hang around here* is great.

   不定詞當名詞用，做主詞。　　　*hang around*　逗留；徘徊
   這句話可説成：*To be here* is great. (在這裡真棒。) 也可
   用 It 當主詞，説成：It's great to hang around here.

2. We've got a lot *to do*.

   不定詞當形容詞用，修飾名詞 lot，這句話天天都可以用，
   可以再加上一句：We have no time to waste. (我們沒有時
   間好浪費。)　　　*have got*　有 (= *have*)

3. I'm impressed *to see so many things*.

   不定詞當副詞用，修飾形容詞 impressed。原則上，不定詞當
   副詞，可修飾動詞、形容詞和副詞，就和一般副詞用法相同。
   I'm impressed 字面意思是「我印象深刻」，在不同句中有不
   同的翻譯，如：Your English is very good.　I'm very
   impressed (你的英文很好。我很佩服。) 在「一口氣背會話」
   p.199 中，有詳細的説明。

4. I *see* a few groups *performing nearby*.

   原則上，*see* + 受詞 + 原形，但是表「無意中看到或聽到」，
   受詞後要用現在分詞做受詞補語，「文法寶典」p.420 中有詳
   細説明。

   【比較】I've never *seen* a band *perform* live. 【特意】
   　　　　(我從未看過樂團現場演出。)
   　　　　live 〔 laɪv 〕 *adv.* 現場地

UNIT 5~8

5. *To tell the truth*, I don't have enough money.

不定詞獨立用法的意思是，不定詞片語和句子的其他部分沒有文法關連，獨立存在，也可說是副詞片語，修飾全句。「文法寶典」p.417 有所有的「獨立不定詞片語」。這個句子可加長為：*To tell the truth*, I don't have enough money with me. (老實說，我身上錢不夠。)

> *to tell the truth* 老實說；坦白說
> = to speak the truth
> = to say the truth

> = to speak frankly
> = to speak sincerely

> = to be plain with you
> = to be candid with you
> = to be frank with you

frankly (ˈfræŋklɪ) *adv.* 坦白地
sincerely (sɪnˈsɪrlɪ) *adv.* 真誠地
plain (plen) *adj.* 坦白的
candid (ˈkændɪd) *adj.* 坦白的

6. I *intended to buy* a smartphone.

【比較】I intended *to have bought* a smartphone.
(我原本打算買一支智慧型手機。)

intended, wished, hoped, promised, meant, expected, planned…	+ to have p.p.

= had │ intended, wished… │ + to V原…

表示過去沒有實現的願望、期待，或計劃。

由於上下文已經說明要借錢買手機，所以不需要用 to have bought 來表示「過去未實現的希望」。如果只是單句：

I intended to buy a smartphone. 並沒有說明過去買了或
沒買。　　　smartphone〔'smart,fon〕*n.* 智慧型手機
cell phone 手機 (= *mobile phone*)

7. Is it possible *for you to lend me some money*?

不定詞做真正主詞，用虛主詞 it 代替，for you 是不定詞意
義上的主詞。【詳見「文法寶典」p.410】

> lend + 間接受詞 + 直接受詞
> borrow + 受詞

8. Would you be kind *enough to help me*?

不定詞當副詞用，修飾相關副詞 enough。enough to… (足
以) 和 too…to… 都是相關修飾詞，成雙成對出現。【詳見
「文法寶典」p.417】

I am ***too*** tired ***to walk*** *any further*.
(我太疲倦了，不能走更遠。)

9. I promise *to pay you back soon*.

不定詞當名詞，做 promise 的受詞。有些動詞只能接不定
詞做受詞。

> promise (答應；保證), agree (同意),
> afford (負擔得起), arrange (安排),　　+ to + 原形
> consent (同意), decide (決定) ……

這類動詞無限多，大致上，表「未來」用不定詞，表「現
在」或「已發生」用動名詞。

TEST *7* 不定詞

選出一個<u>最正確</u>的答案。

( ) 1. My father told me _____ a map for him.
    (A) buy   (B) bought
    (C) to buy   (D) buying

( ) 2. He _____ the man clean the house.
    (A) had   (B) asked   (C) got   (D) told

( ) 3. I saw a boy _____ Mary's room.
    (A) entered   (B) enters
    (C) to enter   (D) enter

( ) 4. We are going to the meeting although we would _____.
    (A) prefer to   (B) prefer not to
    (C) no prefer to   (D) prefer to not

( ) 5. Let me _____ some of the books.
    (A) to help carry   (B) help carrying
    (C) to help to carry   (D) help carry

( ) 6. We should be able to _____ good books from bad ones.
    (A) tell   (B) say
    (C) speak   (D) speaking

(　) 7. _____ into an old friend is a nice surprise.
　　　(A) Ran 　(B) Run 　　(C) To run 　(D) To ran

(　) 8. I prefer to see things _____ read about them.
　　　(A) instead of 　　　(B) rather than
　　　(C) by way of 　　　(D) in order to

(　) 9. She is too young _____ to school.
　　　(A) going 　　　　　(B) to going
　　　(C) go 　　　　　　(D) to go

(　) 10. Mary is _____ go to kindergarten.
　　　(A) enough old to
　　　(B) to enough old
　　　(C) old enough to
　　　(D) to old enough

(　) 11. I haven't decided _____ for my vacation.
　　　(A) where to go
　　　(B) where should I go
　　　(C) to go where
　　　(D) going where

(　) 12. I'm glad _____ of your accomplishments.
　　　(A) hear 　　　　　(B) heard
　　　(C) hearing 　　　　(D) to hear

UNIT 5～8

( ) 13. I have no pen _____.
    (A) to write   (B) to write with
    (C) write   (D) write by

( ) 14. _____ yourself an honest student, you must tell the truth.
    (A) Prove   (B) Having proved
    (C) Proved   (D) To prove

( ) 15. He must be a fool _____.
    (A) to say so   (B) saying so
    (C) said so   (D) in order to say so

【Answers】

1. **C** My father <u>told</u> <u>me</u> ***to buy*** <u>a map</u> *for him*.
    授與動詞 間受   直 接 受 詞
   不定詞片語當 told 的直接受詞，原則上，一個句子有兩個以上的動詞，就可接「不定詞」。

2. **A** 「使役動詞＋受詞＋原形」，使役動詞有：make、let、have 等。
    (B) →He asked the man ***to clean*** the house.
    (C) →He ***got*** the man ***to clean*** the house.
    (D) →He ***told*** the man ***to clean*** the house.

3. **D** 「感官動詞＋受詞＋原形」，感官動詞有：see，hear 等。

4. **B** We are going to the meeting ***although*** *we would* ***prefer*** *not to*.

　　prefer to 是「比較喜歡」，而 prefer not to 是「比較不喜歡」。不定詞的否定，否定字通常放在 to 的前面。

5. **D** let 是使役動詞，接受詞後，加原形動詞。
　　help 是半使役動詞，加 to 或不加 to 都可以，現在英語多不加 to。

　　【比較】Let me ***help carry*** some of the books. 【正，常用】
　　　　　Let me *help to carry* some of the books.
　　　　　【正，少用】

6. **A** ***tell*** A ***from*** B　分辨 A 與 B（= *distinguish A from B*）

7. **C** 偶然遇見老朋友，真令人驚喜。
　　To run into an old friend 是不定詞片語，當主詞。
　　run into 偶然遇見（= *bump into* = *come across*）

8. **B** I ***prefer to*** see things ***rather than*** read about them.
　　prefer to V. ***rather than*** V.　寧願…，也不願～
　　這句話的意思是「我寧願親眼見到，也不願只在書上讀到。」

9. **D** She is *too* young ***to go*** *to school*.

　　不定詞片語當副詞用，修飾副詞 too，表「結果」。
　　too…***to*** V　太…而不能～

10. **C** Mary is ***old enough to*** *go to kindergarten*.

kindergarten（ˈkɪndɚˌɡɑrtn̩）*n.* 幼稚園

不定詞片語當副詞用，修飾 enough，表「結果」。

enough to 足以～

11. **A** I haven't decided ***where to go*** *for my vacation*.

名詞片語，做 decided 的受詞

疑問詞 + 不定詞 = 名詞片語

(B) → where I should go

12. **D** I'm glad ***to hear*** *of your accomplishments*.

我很高興聽到你的成就。

accomplishments（əˈkɑmplɪʃmənts）*n. pl.* 成就；完成

13. **B** I have no pen ***to write with***.

不定詞片語當形容詞用，修飾 pen。

被不定詞所修飾的名詞或代名詞，就是它意義上的受詞，不可重複文法上的受詞。

I have no pen to write with it.（誤）

14. **D** 不定詞片語當副詞用，修飾動詞，表「目的」。

15. **A** He must be a fool *to say so*.（他說這種話，一定是個傻瓜。）

不定詞片語當副詞用，修飾動詞，表「理由」。

【詳見「文法寶典」p.414】

UNIT *8*

動名詞（Gerund）

• •

　　這一回是你和朋友在購物中心（the mall）裡所說的九句話，每一句話都可以主動說出。原則上，動名詞有名詞的功用，做主詞、受詞、同位語、補語等，也有動詞的性質，可接受詞，也可接補語等。

 用背過的語言，說起來最有信心！

Likewise. 我也是。

It has lots of great bargains. 有很多便宜的好東西。

8. 動名詞（Gerund）

I *enjoy being* with you.　　我喜歡和你在一起。

I *appreciate your helping* me.　我很感謝你幫我。

This shop *is worth visiting*.　這家店值得逛逛。

【一、二句意思相連】

I have to *stop walking*.　　我必須停止走路。

How about going to a juice bar?　去果汁店如何？

I don't *feel like eating*.　我不想吃東西。

【二、三句意思相連】

Eating between meals is bad.　吃零食不好。

There is no telling what may happen.　不可能知道會發生什麼事。

I'*m concerned about gaining* weight.　我擔心變胖。

【不吃零食，害怕變胖】

【文法解析】

1. I *enjoy being* with you.

   下列動詞要接動名詞做受詞，不可接不定詞。

   > enjoy（喜歡）、avoid（避免）、finish（完成）、deny
   > （否認）、mind（介意）、resist（抵抗）、appreciate
   > （感激）、practice（練習）

   這類動詞無限多，多表示已發生，詳見「文法寶典」p.436。

2. I *appreciate your helping* me.

   appreciate 後接動名詞做受詞，your 是動名詞意義上的主詞。
   這句話可簡化成：I appreciate your helping.

   > appreciate 原本的意思是「重視」，I appreciate it.
   > 「我重視這件事。」引申為「我很感激。」I appreciate
   > you.「我重視你。」即「我欣賞你。」

   appreciate〔ə'priʃɪˌet〕*v.* 感激；欣賞

3. This shop *is worth visiting*.

   「be worth + V-ing」有三個條件必須遵守：①動名詞為
   主動 ②及物動詞 ③無受詞。

4. I have to *stop walking*.

   > stop + { 不定詞　停下來，去做某事
   > 　　　　 { 動名詞　停止做某事

   I stopped *to eat*. （我停下來去吃東西。）
   I stopped *eating*. （我停止吃東西。）
   類似的動詞還有：remember（記得），forget（忘記）等，
   詳見「文法寶典」p.435, 436。

5. *How about going* to a juice bar?

$$
\left.\begin{array}{l}
\text{How about } (=\textit{How do you feel about}) \\
=\text{What about } (=\textit{What do you think about}) \\
=\text{What do you say to}
\end{array}\right\} + 動名詞？
$$

【詳見「文法寶典」p.148】

6. I don't *feel like eating*.

「feel like + 動名詞」表「想要~」。這句話等於 I don't want to eat.（我不想吃東西。）

7. <u>*Eating between meals*</u> is bad.
　　　　　主　詞

動名詞、不定詞、名詞子句當主詞，要用單數動詞，動名詞可有副詞片語修飾。
meal〔mil〕*n.* 一餐　　*eat between meals* 吃零食

8. *There is no telling* what may happen.

There is no + 動名詞　…是不可能的
　= *It is impossible to* + *V.*
　= *No one can* + *V.*
　= *We cannot* + *V.*

9. I'*m concerned about gaining* weight.

動名詞 gaining 做 about 的受詞，動名詞有動詞性質，所以可接受詞 weight，也可把 gaining weight 當做動名詞片語，做 about 的受詞。
be concerned about 擔心（= *be worried about*）
gain〔gen〕*v.* 增加　　weight〔wet〕*n.* 體重
gain weight 變胖（= *get fat*）

UNIT 5~8

TEST *8* 動名詞

選出一個<u>最正確</u>的答案。

( ) 1. The table is broken. It needs _____.
(A) fix (B) fixed (C) fixing (D) to fix

( ) 2. Have you finished _____ your house?
(A) paint (B) painted
(C) painting (D) to paint

( ) 3. Do you remember _____ the movie I told
you about?
(A) see (B) to see (C) seeing (D) seen

( ) 4. It is true that many of the TV programs are
not worth _____.
(A) seeing (B) being seen
(C) to see (D) to be seen

( ) 5. When did Mary start _____ English?
(A) be learned (B) learning
(C) and learned (D) to be learning

( ) 6. Collecting stamps _____ a good hobby.
(A) are (B) is (C) were (D) have been

( ) 7. We know that _____ on time is important.
(A) is (B) are (C) being (D) been

( ) 8. I hate to interrupt a man when he is busy _____.
(A) working (B) to work
(C) to working (D) worked

( ) 9. Would you mind _____ me your umbrella?
(A) lending (B) to lend
(C) borrow (D) borrowing

( ) 10. I prefer going out _____ at home.
(A) to stay (B) than stay
(C) to staying (D) than staying

( ) 11. I always enjoy _____ fast on the freeway.
(A) to drive (B) drive
(C) to driving (D) driving

( ) 12. It is no use _____ to change it.
(A) trying (B) to try (C) tries (D) to trying

( ) 13. After a long walk, the old man stopped _____ a rest.
(A) taking (B) took (C) take (D) to take

( ) 14. He is good at _____ English.
(A) speak (B) spoke
(C) to speak (D) speaking

( ) 15. You should avoid _____ the same mistake.
(A) making (B) to make
(C) to making (D) to be making

【Answers】

1. **C** *need*, *want*, *require* 作「需要」解時，可用**主動的動名詞**
   代替被動的不定詞。

   $\begin{cases}\end{cases}$ The table *needs fixing*. (這張桌子需要修理。)
   = The table *needs to be fixed*.

2. **C** *finish*, *enjoy*, *mind* 後面接**動名詞**做受詞。
   want, *wish*, *hope*, *decide* 後面接不定詞做受詞。

3. **C** remember 後面接動名詞或不定詞意義不同，**接動名詞表**
   示「記得做過某事」，接不定詞表示「記得要去某事」。

   【比較】 I *remember mailing* this letter.
   （我記得寄了這封信。）
   I will *remember to mail* this letter.
   （我會記得去寄這封信。）

4. **A** 的確有很多電視節目不值得看。
   worth 後面加動名詞，有三個條件必須遵守：①主動的
   ②及物動詞③無受詞。

5. **B** start 和 begin 後面可接不定詞或動名詞，意義相同。

   $\begin{cases}\end{cases}$ start + to V. 開始…
   = start + V-ing

6. **B** 動名詞片語當主詞，動詞用單數。
   collect stamps 集郵   hobby〔ˈhabɪ〕*n.* 嗜好

7. **C** We know *that **being** on time is important.*
   動名詞片語當主詞
   that 引導名詞子句，在子句中 being on time 是 is 的主詞。
   動名詞、不定詞、名詞子句當主詞，動詞用單數。

8. **A** I hate to interrupt a man *when he is busy working.*
（我不喜歡打斷正忙於工作的人。）
be busy 後面省略 in 加動名詞，現在已經不用 *be busy*
in（誤）了。　　interrupt〔͵ɪntəˈrʌpt〕*v.* 打斷

9. **A** *mind + V-ing* 介意…
lend 是授與動詞，後面有兩個受詞，而 borrow 只有一個
受詞。

10. **C** ⎰ *prefer + V-ing* … (*to + V-ing*)
　　⎱ *= prefer to +* 原形動詞… (*rather than +* 原形動詞)
喜歡…不喜歡~；寧願…也不願~【詳見「文法寶典」p.204, 435 】

I prefer going out *to staying* at home.

= I prefer to go out *rather than stay at home.*
（我寧願出去，也不願待在家裡。）
【注意】 rather than 不可接帶 to 的不定詞！

11. **D** *enjoy + V-ing* 喜歡…　　freeway〔ˈfri͵we〕*n.* 高速公路

12. **A** ⎰ *It is no use + V-ing* …是沒有用的
　　⎱ *= There is no use + V-ing*【詳見「文法寶典」p.441 】

13. **D** stop + ⎰ **不定詞** —— 停下來，開始做某事
　　　　　⎱ **動名詞** —— 停止做某事
take a rest 休息一下

14. **D** at 是介系詞，後面接動名詞。　　*be good at* 精通於
這句話也可說成：He is good at spoken English.（他精
通於口說英語。）【spoken〔ˈspokən〕*adj.* 口語的；口頭的】

15. **A** *avoid + V-ing* 避免…

UNIT 9

分 詞（Participle）

 本篇的劇情是：

會叫的狗不咬人。一朝被蛇咬，十年怕草繩。一向沈穩的他竟然向我跑來，我看到他嚇了一跳。他門沒鎖，不知道怎麼辦，我只好找人幫忙。忙得太晚，沒有公車，只好走路。天氣好的時候，我們會再回來。

9. 分 詞 (Participle)

Barking dogs seldom bite.	【諺】會叫的狗不咬人。
A *burnt* child dreads the fire.	【諺】一朝被蛇咬,十年怕草繩。
He *came running* to me.	他向我跑來。
【一、二句是諺語,教人小心】	

Seeing him, I froze on the spot.	看到他,我當場愣住。
He *left* the door *unlocked*.	他門沒鎖。
Not knowing what to do, I asked for help.	不知道該怎麼辦,我找人幫忙。
【嚇一跳——沒鎖門——找人幫忙】	

There being no bus service, we had to walk.	因為沒有公車,我們只好走路。
Weather permitting, we will come back again.	天氣許可的話,我們會再回來。
Generally speaking, the climate here is mild.	一般說來,這裡的氣候很溫和。
【三句話動詞都有 ing,二、三句相關】	

UNIT 9~12

【文法解析】

1. *Barking* dogs seldom bite.

   現在分詞 Barking 當形容詞用，修飾 dogs。類似的有：

   Let *sleeping* dogs lie.【諺】(勿惹是生非。)

   A *rolling* stone gathers no moss.【諺】(滾石不生苔。)

2. A *burnt* child dreads the fire.

   過去分詞 burnt 當形容詞用，修飾 child。如：

   The *lost* chance will never come again. (失去的機會不會再來。)

   dread〔drεd〕v. 害怕，這句話字面意思是「被燙傷的孩子怕火」，引申為「一朝被蛇咬，十年怕草繩」。burn 的三態為：burn–burned–burned/burnt，當形容詞時要用 burnt。

3. He *came running* to me.

   現在分詞 running 當形容詞用，做主詞補語。【詳見「文法寶典」p.14, 453】

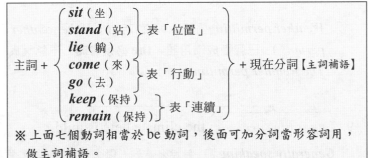

   He *went looking* for his friend. (他去找他的朋友。)

4. *Seeing him*, I froze on the spot.

   Seeing him 是**分詞構句，表時間** (= *When I saw him*)。

   freeze〔friz〕v. 結冰；呆住不動　　*on the spot* 當場

5. He *left* the door *unlocked*.

過去分詞 unlocked **當形容詞用，做受詞補語，修飾** door。
【詳見「文法寶典」p.453】

6. *Not knowing what to do*, I asked for help.

Not knowing what do to 是**分詞構句，表原因**（= *Because
I did not know what to do*）。否定詞 Not 要放在分詞前，副
詞子句改分詞構句的方法，詳見「文法寶典」p.458。
ask (*sb.*) ***for help*** 請（某人）幫忙

7. *There being no bus service*, we had to walk.

There is 或 There are 的分詞形式是 ***There being***。
這句話源自：Because there was no bus service, ...

8. *Weather permitting*, we will come back again.

Weather permitting「天氣許可的話」（= *If the weather
permits*），已經變成慣用語，**the 必須省略**，不能說成
The weather permitting（誤）。

9. *Generally speaking*, the climate here is mild.

Generally speaking「一般說來」是「獨立分詞構句」，意義
上的主詞表示一般人，不以主要子句的主詞為主詞。其他
還有：***frankly speaking***（坦白地說）、***roughly speaking***
（大致說來）、***strictly speaking***（嚴格地說）、***properly
speaking***（正確地說）等。【詳見「文法寶典」p.463】
climate〔'klaɪmɪt〕*n.* 氣候　　mild〔maɪld〕*adj.* 溫和的

TEST 9 分 詞

選出一個最正確的答案。

( ) 1. The man _____ by the car got a broken leg.
(A) hit (B) hitting (C) was hit (D) who hit

( ) 2. Do you hear the noise _____ by the children playing outside?
(A) making (B) made
(C) make (D) which made

( ) 3. When I walked into the room, I found her _____ at the desk.
(A) siting (B) seating (C) sat (D) seated

( ) 4. A book _____ the meanings of words is called a dictionary.
(A) gives (B) gived (C) gave (D) giving

( ) 5. The books _____ from the library have been returned.
(A) borrow (B) borrowing
(C) borrowed (D) to be borrowed

( ) 6. He is going to have his coat _____.
(A) making (B) make (C) made (D) to make

( ) 7. I've never seen a _____ parrot.
(A) singing (B) sang (C) sung (D) sing

(   ) 8. _____ food must be kept in the freezer.

    (A) To freeze   (B) Froze

    (C) Freeze   (D) Frozen

(   ) 9. The boy _____ is Henry.

    (A) wearing a torn coat

    (B) wears a torn coat

    (C) worn a tearing coat

    (D) wearing a tearing coat

(   ) 10. There are many boys and girls _____ in the park now.

    (A) picnics   (B) picnicing

    (C) picnicking   (D) picnicked

(   ) 11. I saw him _____.

    (A) walked into the room

    (B) to eat a banana   (C) was crying

    (D) running across the street

(   ) 12. Mr. Smith had the man _____ the box out of his office.

    (A) take   (B) takes   (C) took   (D) taken

(   ) 13. Repeat after me _____.

    (A) with your books closed

    (B) with your books closing

    (C) with your closing books

    (D) with closing your books

( ) 14. He came to the hospital with his arm _____.
　　　(A) broken　(B) break　(C) breaks　(D) broke

( ) 15. The money _____ in the closet was found.
　　　(A) which hid　　　(B) hidden
　　　(C) hiding　　　　(D) was hidden

【Answers】

1. **A**　The man *hit by the car* got a broken leg.

= The man *who was hit by the car* got a broken leg.

（被汽車撞到的那個人，斷了一條腿。）

「形容詞子句」變成「形容詞片語」：①去關代②去 be 動詞。

2. **B**　Do you hear the noise *made by the children playing*

outside?

= Do you hear the noise *which is made by the children*

playing outside?

（你有聽到在外面玩的小孩製造的噪音嗎？）

3. **D**　*When I walked into the room*, I found her *seated* at the desk.

雖然 Be seated. = Seat yourself. = Sit down.（坐下），

但在此不能用 seated herself，避免和 her 重複。可説

成：..., I found her *sitting* at the desk.

> 【注意】 要寫成 sitting，有兩個 t，單音節的字，單子音
> 字母，須重複子音。【詳見「文法寶典」p.286】

4. **D**　A book *giving* the meanings of words is called a dictionary.

= A book *which* gives the meanings of words is called a dictionary.

（解釋字的意思的書，被稱爲字典。）

形容詞子句改成分詞片語：① 去關代 ② V→V-ing。

5. **C**　The books *borrowed* from the library have been returned.

= The books *which* were borrowed from the library have been returned.

（從圖書館借來的書已經被歸還。）

6. **C**　「have + 非人 + p.p.」表「自己不做而讓別人做」。

coat 是「外套」，overcoat 是「大衣」。

7. **A**　a singing parrot　一隻會唱歌的鸚鵡

singing 是現在分詞，當形容詞用。

parrot〔ˈpærət〕*n.* 鸚鵡【sparrow〔ˈspæro〕*n.* 麻雀】

8. **D**　*frozen food* 冷凍食物

9. **A**　The boy *wearing* a torn coat is Henry.

= The boy *who* wears a torn coat is Henry.

（穿著破外套的那個小男孩是亨利。）

tear〔tɛr〕*v.* 撕裂【三態變化：tear–tore–torn】

wear（穿）【三態變化：wear–wore–worn】

10. **C**　There are many boys and girls *picnicking in the park now*.

picnic〔'pɪknɪk〕*v.* 野餐【三態變化為：picnic–picnicked–picnicked，現在分詞為 picnicking】

字尾是 c，而發音為 /k/ 時，則加上字母 k 再加 ed 或 ing，純粹為了發音方便。【詳見「文法寶典」p.286】

11. **D**　I saw him *running across the street*. (我看到他跑過街道。)

感官動詞＋受詞＋現在分詞（做受詞補語）

(A) →I saw him walking into the room.

(B) →I saw him eating a banana.

(C) →I saw him crying.

12. **A**　使役動詞 had ＋受詞＋原形動詞。

13. **A**　Repeat after me *with your books closed*.

（把你們的書合起來，跟著我唸。）

| with　　 ⎫ |
| without ⎭ ＋受詞＋分詞 |，表示伴隨著主要動詞的情況。

因為 books 是「非人」，所以用過去分詞 closed。

repeat〔rɪ'pit〕*v.* 重複；重說；重唸

14. **A**　He came to the hospital *with his arm broken*.

（他來到醫院，手臂摔斷了。）【文法分析見第 13 題。】

15. **B**　The money *hidden in the closet* was found.

＝ The money *which was hidden in the closet* was found.

hide〔haɪd〕*v.* 隱藏【三態變化為：hide–hid–hid/hidden】

closet〔'klɑzɪt〕*n.* 衣櫥

UNIT *10*

假設法（Subjunctive Mood）

· ·

　　英文表達思想的方式有直說法、假設法、命令句三種。直說法有 12 種時態，敘述事實，假設法有三種時態，即與現在事實、過去事實，和未來事實相反，命令句只有一種時態。有些直說法和命令句中有 if 子句，不一定是假設法，非常複雜，背句子最簡單。

 下面都是你可以和外國朋友說的話，你是主動的。

1.

I agree.

If he promised to help, he will do it.

2.

Me too.

I wish I were as smart as he.

3.

If I had been more careful, I might not be in trouble.

You're probably right.

UNIT 9〜12

10. 假設法（Subjunctive Mood）

If he *promised* to help, he *will do* it.	如果他答應幫忙，他就會做。
I wish I *were* as smart as he.	我希望我和他一樣聰明。
If I *had been* more careful, I *might* not *be* in trouble.	如果我再小心一點，我就不會有麻煩了。
【找聰明人幫忙，因為自己不小心】	

He talked *as if* he knew everything.	他說話的樣子好像他什麼都知道。
He *suggested* that we *check* again.	他建議我們再檢查一次。
It's about time we *left*.	我們該走了。
【一、二句相關連】	

Should it rain, we have to stay here.	萬一下雨，我們就必須留在這裡。
I *would* be happy *to go with you*.	如果能和你一起去，我會很高興。
Failing this, what will you do?	如果不行，你要做什麼？
【二、三句相關連】	

UNIT 9~12

【文法解析】

1. If he *promised* to help, he *will do* it.【直説法】

   傳統文法書假設法公式：

$$
\text{If} + \text{S} + \text{V}\cdots,\ \text{S} + \left\{ \begin{array}{l} \text{shall} \\ \text{will} \end{array} \right\} + \text{V}\cdots\ \text{【錯誤公式，只有部分適用】}
$$

   If you are right, I am wrong.

$$
\text{If} + \text{S} + \text{過去式動詞}\cdots,\ \text{S} + \left\{ \begin{array}{l} \text{could} \\ \text{would} \\ \text{should} \\ \text{might} \end{array} \right\} + \text{V}\cdots
$$

   【錯誤公式，只有部分適用】

   假設法的要點：

   ① could, would, should, might 是假設法助動詞。

   ② if + S + 過去式動詞，可能表假設法現在式，也可能表直説法過去式。

   ③ if + S + had p.p. 是假設法過去式。

   ④ 想説什麼就説什麼，不要受公式限制，心中認爲眞實用直説法，心中認爲是假的，才用假設法。

   If he promises to help, he will do it.【直説法】
   If he promised to help, he would do it.【假設法】
   If he promised to help, he will do it.【直説法】

2. I wish I *were* as smart as he.

$$
\text{S} + \text{wish (that)} + \text{S} \left\{ \begin{array}{l} \text{過去式或 were} \longrightarrow \text{指現在} \\ \text{過去完成式} \longrightarrow \text{指過去} \\ \text{過去式助動詞} + \text{原形} \longrightarrow \text{指未來} \end{array} \right.
$$

UNIT 9～12

$$
\text{I wish I} \begin{cases} \textbf{\textit{were}} \text{ there now.（我真希望我現在在那裡。）} \\ \textbf{\textit{had been}} \text{ there yesterday.} \\ \text{（我真希望我昨天去過那裡。）} \\ \textbf{\textit{could be}} \text{ there tomorrow.} \\ \text{（我真希望我明天能去那裡。）} \end{cases}
$$

3. If I *had been* more careful, I *might* not *be* in trouble.

假設法或直說法的時態看主要子句,「might + 原形」是假設法的現在式或未來式。

【比較】If I had been more careful, I **might** not **have been** in trouble.

（如果我過去小心一點,我過去就不會有麻煩了。）

—— 假設法過去式

4. He talked *as if* he knew everything.

as if 後面可接直說法和假設法,這句話是直說法過去式。【詳見「文法寶典」p.371】

【比較】He **talks as if** he **knew** everything.【假設法現在式】

5. He *suggested* that we *check* again.

suggest（建議）, advise（建議）, demand（要求）, command（命令）, order（命令）, propose（提議）, request（要求）, require（要求）, insist（堅持）, recommend（建議）, ask（要求）......	+ that...(should) + 原形

上面是**慾望動詞**,有無限多,凡是建議、命令、要求別人「應該」做某事,就要用假設法動詞,因為「應做而未做」。【詳見「文法寶典」p.372】

6. *It's about time* we *left*.

這句話原來是：It's about time (that) we left. 現在 that 已經不用。意思是「我們該走了」，事實上還沒有，所以用假設法動詞 left。極少人用 It's about time we (*should*) leave.

7. *Should* it rain, we have to stay here.

Should it rain 來自 If it should rain，表示未來可能性極小的假設，should 作「萬一」解。主要子句可用直說法、假設法或命令句，本句是直說法未來式，have to 可表現在或未來。

8. I *would* be happy *to go with you*.

不定詞片語可代替 if 子句，這句話也可說成：I would be happy if I could go with you.，用 would 和 could 是表示客氣，因為說話者認為不該問，才用假設法助動詞。【詳見「文法寶典」p.366】

9. *Failing this*, what will you do?

分詞片語可代替 if 子句，這句話是直說法未來式，相當於：If this fails, what will you do?
Failing this 要當成慣用語看，作「如果不行」解，根據上下文，這句話的意思是：If I don't go with you, what will you do?

TEST *10* 假設法

選出一個最<u>正確</u>的答案。

(   ) 1. If I _____ with him, I would have missed my classes.
    (A) had gone   (B) have gone
    (C) went   (D) gone

(   ) 2. We wished she _____ sick yesterday.
    (A) isn't   (B) wasn't
    (C) weren't   (D) hadn't been

(   ) 3. If your mother _____ a doctor, she wouldn't be so busy.
    (A) isn't   (B) is   (C) weren't   (D) aren't

(   ) 4. If the sun _____ in the west, I would help you.
    (A) rises   (B) were to rise
    (C) is to rise   (D) rose

(   ) 5. He could _____ the prize if he had run faster.
    (A) wins   (B) won
    (C) have won   (D) be won

(   ) 6. James talks as if he _____ everthing.
    (A) knowing   (B) knew
    (C) know   (D) were known

( ) 7. If he promised to be here yesterday, he _____ certainly come today.

(A) will   (B) can   (C) would   (D) could

( ) 8. Isn't it high time you _____ to bed?

(A) are going   (B) will go

(C) have gone   (D) went

( ) 9. If only I _____ there at that time.

(A) was   (B) were

(C) should be   (D) had been

( ) 10. It looks _____ it might rain.

(A) this   (B) as   (C) as if   (D) that

( ) 11. This young lady behaves as though she _____ an old woman.

(A) is   (B) was

(C) were   (D) has been

( ) 12. I propose that he _____ chairman.

(A) electing   (B) elected

(C) elects   (D) be elected

( ) 13. Had he gone there, he _____ her.

(A) had seen   (B) saw

(C) would have seen   (D) will have seen

UNIT 9~12

( ) 14. If I had studied medicine, I _____ a doctor now.
    (A) would be   (B) was
    (C) would have been   (D) had been

( ) 15. If the room is dark, _____ on the light.
    (A) to turn   (B) turning   (C) turn   (D) turns

【Answers】

1. **A**   If I *had gone* with him, I *would have missed* my classes.
這條題目是假設法過去式，If 子句中用 had + p.p.，表「與過去相反」，主要子句 would have + p.p.。

2. **D**   wish 後是不可能的希望，用過去完成式表示與過去事實相反。
    【比較】 We wish she *weren't* sick now.—— 與現在事實相反
                【詳見「文法寶典」p.368】

3. **C**   假設法的現在式，If 子句用過去式或 were。

4. **B**   If 子句可用 were to + 原形，為假設法的未來式。

5. **C**   同第 1 題。

6. **B**   James talks *as if he knew everything.*
as if 後可以用直說法和假設法，本句是與現在事實相反的假設法，表示他不可能知道一切；如果說話者認為是真的，就用直說法，說成：James talks *as if he knows* everything.

7. **A** 這句話是直說法。【詳見「文法寶典」p.357】

8. **D** 詳見本回第 6 句文法說明。

9. **D** 但願我當時在那裡。
   if only 表「願望」，用假設法。【詳見「文法寶典」p.370】

10. **C** as if 引導副詞子句，表示與未來事實相反，這句話的意思是「天看起來好像要下雨」，但事實上說話者認為不會下雨。【詳見「文法寶典」p.371】

11. **C** as though = as if，後面接過去式動詞或 were，表示與現在事實相反。
    behave〔bɪ'hev〕*v.* 行為；舉止

12. **D** propose「提議」，和 suggest「建議」、insist「堅持」一樣，是慾望動詞，that 子句省略 should。
    elect〔ɪ'lɛkt〕*v.* 選舉　　chairman〔'tʃɛrmən〕*n.* 主席

13. **C** *Had* he gone there = *If* he *had* gone there。

14. **A** If I *had studied* medicine, I *would be* a doctor now.
    If 子句和主要子句時態可依實際情況而定。【詳見「文法寶典」p.364】

15. **C** 如果房間很暗，就把燈打開。
    If 子句可和命令句連用。
    If 子句可能是直說法，敘述事實，也可能是假設法，與事實相反。【詳見「文法寶典」p.356】

UNIT 9~12

UNIT 11
it 和 there 的用法

• •

　　it 可以表天氣、時間、距離等，也可以代替不定詞和 that 子句，做形式上的主詞或受詞。There is 和 There are 的主詞在後面，動詞 is 或 are 要看主詞而定。

 你很熱情，喜歡說英文。你想邀請外國朋友吃飯。

UNIT 9~12

11. it 和 there 的用法

What time is *it*?	現在幾點鐘？
How far is *it* from here to downtown?	從這裡到市區有多遠？
It was kind *of you* to tell me this.	感謝你告訴我。

【背誦技巧：三句話都有 it】

See to *it that* your bag is safe.	好好注意你的袋子。
It seems *that* the weather is getting better.	天氣似乎變好了。
It happens *that* I'm free this afternoon.	剛好我今天下午有空。

【三句話都有 it 和 that】

There are a few good restaurants around here.	這附近有幾家不錯的餐廳。
There is no need for us to make a reservation.	我們不需要預約。
I find *it* pleasant to spend time with you.	我發覺和你在一起很愉快。

【一、二句相關，都有 there】

【文法解析】

1. What time is *it*?

   it 可以指**時間**、**天氣**、**距離**等，做主詞。

   > *It* is ten o'clock. (現在十點鐘。)
   > *It* is still early. (時間還早。)

2. How far is *it from here to downtown*?

   it 指**距離**。from here to downtown 是介詞片語，當副詞片語用，修飾動詞 is。

   > *It* is a ten-minute walk. (步行十分鐘。)

3. *It* was kind *of you to tell me this*.

   it 代替不定詞片語，of you 是不定詞意義上的主詞。

   It is...of *sb.* to 的句型，用於對 of 後的受詞稱讚或責備時，如 polite (有禮貌的)、careful (小心的)、nice (好的)、bold (大膽的)、silly (愚蠢的) 等，詳見「文法寶典」p.410。

   一般情形用：It is...for *sb.* to 的句型，如：

   > *It* is difficult *for you* to read this book.
   > (你要讀這本書很困難。)

4. See to *it that your bag is safe*.

   it 可以**代替 that 子句**，做介系詞 to 的受詞，因為原則上，that 子句不能做介系詞的受詞。see to 是一個成語，字面意思是「看著」，引申為「注意」，這句話也可說成：***See that*** your bag is safe.。

UNIT 9～12

5. *It* <u>seems</u> *that the weather is getting better.*
   完全不及物動詞

   > ***It seems that~*** 的句型中，It 為形式主詞，that 子句為真
   > 正主詞，seem 是完全不及物動詞，這句話也常説成：It
   > seems to me that the weather is getting better. (我覺得
   > 天氣似乎變好了。) 類似的還有 appear (似乎)，happen
   > (剛好) 等。

6. *It* <u>happens</u> *that I'm free this afternoon.*
   完全不及物動詞

   happen〔'hæpən〕*v.* 發生；碰巧；剛好

7. *There are* a few good <u>restaurants</u> *around here.*

   There is, There are 的主詞要看後面的名詞，restaurants
   是複數，所以用 are。

8. *There is* no need for us to make a reservation.

   need 是單數，用 There is。
   reservation〔,rɛzə'veʃən〕*n.* 預約

9. I find *it* pleasant to spend time *with you.*

   it 代替不定詞片語，做受詞，pleasant 是受詞補語。
   pleasant〔'plɛznt〕*adj.* 愉快的 (= *giving pleasure*)

TEST *11* it 和 there 的用法

選出一個<u>最正確</u>的答案。

(　) 1. This made _____ easier for him to understand his patients.
(A) there　(B) one　(C) it　(D) that

(　) 2. We think _____ our duty to pay taxes to our government.
(A) that　(B) this　(C) its　(D) it

(　) 3. I make _____ a rule to get up at seven every morning.
(A) that　(B) it　(C) one　(D) which

(　) 4. Was _____ you who sent me the box?
(A) it　(B) he　(C) which　(D) what

(　) 5. I found _____ impossible to go on with my work.
(A) that　(B) it　(C) one　(D) which

(　) 6. It _____ that he devoted himself to his studies.
(A) seems　(B) makes　(C) finds　(D) takes

(　) 7. I owe _____ to you that I have succeeded.
(A) that　(B) this　(C) it　(D) what

(   ) 8. _____ a lot of houses destroyed by the gas explosion.

    (A) There were   (B) There had

    (C) They are   (D) They had

(   ) 9. You have done your best. _____ no need for you to apologize.

    (A) It is   (B) There is

    (C) There are   (D) That is

(   ) 10. I _____ that he would accept my offer.

    (A) took it granted   (B) took it for granted

    (C) took it for sure   (D) took for granted

(   ) 11. _____ he has worked out a solution to his problems.

    (A) He appears that

    (B) It appears to me that

    (C) It happened that

    (D) It happens to me that

(   ) 12. It _____ me five minutes to walk to the station.

    (A) makes   (B) costs   (C) spends   (D) takes

(   ) 13. It was kind _____ you to warn me against the danger.

    (A) on   (B) with   (C) of   (D) for

(　) 14. _____ little whether you go by bus or by train.

    (A) It matters　　　　(B) It makes

    (C) It takes　　　　　(D) It has

(　) 15. It was _____ I heard of Linda.

    (A) not long　　　　　(B) not long before

    (C) not before long　　(D) before not long

【Answers】

1. **C**　This made ***it*** easier *for him to understand his patients.*

    這使他更容易了解他的病人。

    patient〔ˋpeʃənt〕*n.* 病人　*adj.* 有耐心的

    it 是虛受詞，代替不定詞片語，easier 是受詞補語。

2. **D**　我們認為繳稅給政府是我們的義務。

    duty〔ˋdjutɪ〕*n.* 義務；責任

    it 是虛受詞，代替不定詞片語，our duty 是受詞補語。

3. **B**　I make ***it*** a rule *to get up at seven every morning.*

    make it a rule「通常」，*it* 代替後面的不定詞片語。

4. **A**　用 *it* 加強語氣。【詳見「文法寶典」p.115】

5. **B**　I found ***it*** impossible *to go on with my work.*

    我覺得不可能繼續做我的工作。

    it 代替不定詞片語做虛受詞。

6. **A** It <u>seems</u> *that he devoted himself to his studies.*
他似乎專心於他的學業。

It 代替後面的 that 子句，做虛主詞。

    ⎧ *It seems that* 似乎
    ⎩ = *It appears that*

    devote oneself *to* 專心於

7. **C** I owe <u>it</u> to you *that I have succeeded.*
我的成功要歸功於你。

it 是虛受詞，代替 that 子句。   *owe…to~* 把…歸功於~

8. **A** *there is* 和 *there are* 的過去式是 *there was* 和 *there were*。
主詞 houses 是複數，故用 were。

There *were* a lot of <u>houses</u> destroyed by the gas explosion.
                     主詞

（有很多的房子在氣爆中被摧毀。）

9. **B** *There is no need…* 沒有必要；不需要…【詳見「文法寶典」p.323】
此時 need 是名詞。   apologize〔ə'pɑlə,dʒaɪz〕*v.* 道歉

10. **B** I took <u>it</u> for granted *that he would accept my offer.*
我認為他接受我的提議是理所當然的。

it 是受詞，代替 that 子句。

take sth. for granted 認為某事為理所當然
for 在此相當於 to be。也可能源自：take *sth.* for
sth. granted，第二個 sth. 省略。

grant〔grænt〕*v.* 同意；承認

11. **B** It appears to me ***that*** he has worked out a solution to his

problems. 我覺得他似乎已經想出問題的解決辦法。

appear〔ə'pɪr〕v. 似乎；看起來；出現
work out 想出；解決
It appears to me that··· 我覺得似乎···

12. **D** ***It*** 當主詞，花費時間用 take，花費金錢用 cost，人當主詞，用 spend。

13. **C** 你眞好，警告我注意危險。

It 代替後面的不定詞片語。不定詞片語的意義上主詞，正常情況用 ***for you***，在此表示稱讚，用 ***of you***。

14. **A** ***It*** <u>matters</u> little ***whether*** you go by bus or by taxi.
完全不及物動詞

你搭公車或火車去，都沒什麼關係。
It 代替 whether 子句，做虛主詞。
matter〔'mætɚ〕v. 重要；關係重大

15. **B** It was ***not long before*** I heard of Linda.
我不久就聽到琳達的事。
= I heard of Linda ***before long***.

hear of 是「聽說」，***hear from*** 是「接到···的信息」。
It was not long before··· 不久···
before long 也做「不久」解，但是是副詞片語。
【詳見「文法寶典」p.495】

UNIT *12*

關係代名詞（Relative Pronouns）

•••••••••••••••••••••••••••••••••••••

　　關係代名詞＝代名詞＋連接詞，主要分為簡單關係代名詞（who, whose, whom, which, of which, that），和複合關係代名詞（what, whatever, whoever, whosever, whomever, whichever）。

　　　　簡單關係代名詞——引導形容詞子句
　　　　複合關係代名詞——引導名詞子句或副詞子句

所謂複合，就是二個以上的字結合，如 what = the thing that，whoever = anyone who 或 no matter who。

 這一回是你和外國人在餐廳裡講的話，你很熱情，英文說個不停，外國人只有聽你的。

1. All that glitters is not gold. — No, it's not.

2. The man you see there is a famous chef. — Wow.

3. He is what is called a genius. — He must be smart.

UNIT 9～12

12. 關係代名詞
（Relative Pronouns）

All *that* glitters is not gold.

The man *you see there* is a famous chef.

He is *what is called* a genius.

【背誦技巧：人不可貌相——那個人是名廚、天才】

【諺】發光的未必都是金子。

你在那裡看到的人是一位名廚。

他就是所謂的天才。

You can order *whatever* you want.

This is the dish *which* I mentioned before.

The food tastes great, and, *what is better*, it is healthy.

【三句相關，強調食物】

你想吃什麼就點什麼。

這就是我之前提過的那道菜。

這個食物很好吃，更棒的是，又很健康。

I spend *what money* I have on food.

You are *what* you eat.

I am a person *who* enjoys fine food.

【三句話都提到食物】

我所有的錢都用在食物上。

吃什麼，就長成什麼樣子。

我是喜歡美食的人。

【文法解析】

1. All *that glitters* is not gold.

   先行詞有 *all, the only, the same, the very, the first, no,*
   every 等時，關代常用 that。在句中，關係代名詞 that，引
   導形容詞子句，修飾 All，在子句中，that 有代名作用，做
   glitters 的主詞。All...not... 是部分否定，這句話字面意思
   是「發光的東西不全部都是金子。」引申為「中看的未必中用；
   金玉其外，敗絮其中；人不可貌相。」　　glitter〔ˈglɪtɚ〕*v.* 發光

2. The man *you see there* is a famous chef.

   省略了關代 that 或 whom 的形容詞子句，修飾 The man，
   在子句中，省略的關代做 see 的受詞。**關代做受詞時常省**
   略，尤其是在口語中。
   chef〔ʃɛf〕*n.* 主廚【這個字來自法文，ch 唸 /ʃ/】

3. He is *what is called* a genius.

   what is called「所謂的」是一個插入語，所謂插入語，就
   是和句中其他文法沒有關連，也可以用 *what we call* 或
   what you call 來代替。在文法上，這個片語屬於複合關
   代 what 的慣用語。【詳見「文法寶典」p.157】
   genius〔ˈdʒinjəs〕*n.* 天才

4. You can order <u>*whatever you want*</u>.
   名詞子句

   複合關代 whatever 引導名詞子句，做 order 的受詞，在子
   句中，whatever 又做 want 的受詞，whatever 在此等於
   anything that。

5. This is the dish *which* I *mentioned before*.

關代 which 引導形容詞子句，修飾 dish，子句中 which 做 mentioned 的受詞，which 可以省略，也可用 that 代替。

6. The food tastes great, and, *what is better*, it is healthy.

複合關代 what 的慣用語 *what is better*「更好的是」，在句中做插入語。【詳見「文法寶典」p.157 和 p.654】

7. I spend *what money I have* on food.
名詞子句

= I spend *what I have* on food.
名詞子句

複合關係形容詞 what，加上所修飾的字，等於複合關係代名詞，句中 what money 等於 what。

I will give you *what books I possess*. (我會給你我所有的書。)
名詞子句

what 可用 whatever 來加強語氣。【詳見「文法寶典」p.158】

8. You are *what you eat*.
名詞子句

what 引導名詞子句，做主詞補語；在子句中，what 做 eat 的受詞。這句話是慣用句，意思是「吃得好就長得好；吃得差就長不好。」你的飲食對你的外表有很大的影響。

9. I am a person *who enjoys fine food*.

關代 who 引導形容詞子句，修飾先行詞 a person，在子句中做 enjoys 的主詞，所以用主格 who。
enjoy〔ɪn'dʒɔɪ〕v. 享受；喜愛；樂於

TEST *12* 關係代名詞

選出一個<u>最正確</u>的答案。

(　) 1. The chair _____ he is sitting is very good.
 (A) on which   (B) on that
 (C) which   (D) that

(　) 2. Do you know the man to _____ I spoke?
 (A) that (B) who (C) whom (D) which

(　) 3. He is the only man _____ I want to see.
 (A) what (B) whom (C) which (D) that

(　) 4. I like the house _____ he lives.
 (A) which   (B) that
 (C) in which   (D) in where

(　) 5. The magazine _____ you lent me is very interesting.
 (A) who (B) which (C) what (D) whom

(　) 6. Water is to fish _____ air is to man.
 (A) that (B) which (C) what (D) so

(　) 7. Eat _____ food you like.
 (A) whatever (B) which (C) that (D) where

(　) 8. You are all _____ a teacher should be.
 (A) who (B) that (C) what (D) which

(   ) 9. The man _____ son has returned from Japan looks happy.

    (A) his   (B) who   (C) whose   (D) whom

(   ) 10. The village _____ I visited last year is a very quiet place.

    (A) which (B) where (C) when   (D) whom

(   ) 11. _____ we should do is make our world peaceful.

    (A) That   (B) What   (C) Those   (D) Which

(   ) 12. Is this the child _____ you saw in the park?

    (A) who   (B) whose (C) which   (D) what

(   ) 13. Taipei is the most interesting city _____ I have ever visited.

    (A) that   (B) when   (C) whom   (D) where

(   ) 14. The man gave me all the money _____ he had.

    (A) when   (B) that   (C) whose   (D) what

(   ) 15. There is no rule _____ has exceptions.

    (A) which (B) that   (C) as   (D) but

【Answers】

1. A   The chair on *which he is sitting* is very good.

關係代名詞 *which* 引導形容詞子句，在子句中做 on 的受詞。

2. **C**　Do you know the man *to **whom** I spoke*?
關係代名詞 **whom** 引導形容詞子句，修飾 the man，在子句中做 to 的受詞，所以是受格 **whom**。

3. **D**　先行詞有 the only 修飾，用**關代 that**。

4. **C**　I like the house *in **which** he lives*.

= I like the house ***which** he lives in*.

= I like the house ***where** he lives*.
關係代名詞有代名詞作用，但關係副詞沒有。

5. **B**　The magazine ***which** you lent me* is very interesting.
關係代名詞 **which** 引導形容詞子句，修飾 magazine，在子句中，**which** 做 lent 的直接受詞，因為是「非人」，所以用 **which**。

6. **C**　水之於魚，猶如空氣之於人。

A is to **B** $\left\{ \begin{array}{c} \textbf{\textit{what}} \\ \textbf{\textit{as}} \end{array} \right\}$ **C** is to **D**.　A 之於 B，猶如 C 之於 D。

7. **A**　Eat ***whatever** food you like*.
複合關係形容詞 **whatever** 引導名詞子句，做 Eat 的受詞。在子句中，whatever 修飾 food。複合關係形容詞 + 名詞 = 複合關係代名詞這句話也可說成：Eat **whatever** you like. 或 Eat **what** you like.（想吃什麼就吃什麼。）
whatever 和 what 既是複合關係代名詞，也是複合關係形容詞，所謂「複合」就是由兩個以上的字所組成的字。

8. **B**　You are all ***that** a teacher should be*.　你是個教師的典型。
當補語的關代，一定要用 that。【詳見「文法寶典」p.155】
句中的 **that** 也可省略。

9. **C** The man ⌒*whose son has returned from Japan* looks happy.

   whose 是關代所有格，也是形容詞，引導形容詞子句，修飾 The man，在子句中，修飾 son。

10. **A** The village ⌒*which I visited last year* is a very quiet place.

    關代 *which* 引導形容詞子句，修飾 The village，在子句中，*which* 做 visited 的受詞。形容詞子句若是完整句，才能用關係副詞。

11. **B** **What** we should do is make our world peaceful.

    名詞子句

    複合關係代名詞 **What** 引導名詞子句，做 is 的主詞，在子句中，**What** 做 do 的受詞。　　**What = The thing that**

12. **A** *who you saw* 是形容詞子句，修飾 the child。

    從前用 whom，現在用 who 或 that，並且可以省略。

    【比較】　Is this the child
    {
    　you saw【最常用】
    　that you saw【第二常用】
    　who you saw【第三常用】
    　whom you saw【現在不用】
    }
    in the park?

13. **A** 先行詞前有最高級，關係代名詞用 *that*。

14. **B** The man gave <u>me</u> <u>all the money</u> ⌒*that he had*.

    間受　　　直受

    先行詞前有 all，關係代名詞用 *that*。

15. **D** 沒有規則沒有例外；有規則就有例外。

    先行詞前有 *no*，關代用 *but*，此時，*but* 等於 *that…not*，為雙重否定的用法。【詳見「文法寶典」p.160】

UNIT *13*

副詞子句（Adverbial Clause）

• •

　　從屬子句有三種：名詞子句、形容詞子句、副詞子句。副詞子句和副詞一樣，可以修飾動詞、形容詞、副詞。修飾動詞時，可表動作的時間、地點、狀態、比較、原因、目的、結果、條件、讓步等，歸納的目的是便於翻譯和記憶。

　　你是這一回的主角，帶你的外國朋友去吃飯、看電影。

Me either. 是 I couldn't stop, either. 的省略。

13. 副詞子句（Adverbial Clause）

Although this place is crowded,
  we still found a table.
It is as good *as* I expected.
The food is so great *that* I
  will be back soon.

【背誦技巧：進了餐廳，坐在餐桌旁開
  始説】

雖然這個地方很擠，
我們還是找到一桌。
這和我預期的一樣好。
這食物太好吃了，我
很快會再來。

Once I started eating it, I
  couldn't stop.
As time goes by, I prefer light
  meals.
Unless you eat more now,
  you will be hungry later.

【吃了一口，就開始説】

我一吃就上癮。

隨著年齡增長，我比
較喜歡清淡的餐點。
除非你現在多吃一點，
否則你待會兒會餓。

Let's go *if* you're done.
Now that we are here, how
  about seeing a movie?
Whatever movie you like,
  it's fine with me.

【吃完飯後説】

如果你吃完我們就走。
既然我們在這裡，看
場電影如何？
無論你喜歡什麼電影，
我都可以。

UNIT 13~16

【文法解析】

1. *Although this place is crowded*, we still found a table.

   although 引導表「**讓步**」的副詞子句，修飾 found。所謂表「讓步」，就是對主要子句加以退讓，其他還有：*even if*（即使），*whether…or*（無論），*notwithstanding that*（雖然），*when*（雖然），*though*（雖然）。在中文中，「雖然」後往往接「但是」，但英文只能用一個連接詞。【詳見「文法寶典」p.524】

   Although this place is crowded, *but* we found a table.（誤）

2. It is *as* good *as I expected*.

   as 引導副詞子句，表「**比較**」，修飾前面的 as，句中第一個 as 是副詞，修飾 good，第二個 as 才是連接詞。*as…as* 是相關修飾詞，必須成雙成對出現。【詳見「文法寶典」p.502】

3. The food is *so* great *that I'll be back soon*.

   that 引導副詞子句，修飾相關修飾詞 so，表「**結果**」，so 修飾 great。表「結果」的連接詞有：*so…that*，*such…that*，*so (that)* 等。【詳見「文法寶典」p.516】

4. *Once I started eating it*, I couldn't stop.

once 可以翻成「一旦」或「一…就」，引導副詞子句，修飾主要動詞 stop。once 可表示「**時間**」或「**條件**」。這句話是直說法過去式，could 是 can 的過去式。【詳見「文法寶典」p.494】

5. *As time goes by*, I prefer light meals.

句中的 *As time goes by = As time goes on*，字面意思是「隨著時間的過去」，引申為「隨著年齡增長」(= *As I get older*)。as 引導副詞子句，表「**時間**」，修飾動詞 prefer。連接詞 as 可表「**原因**」、「**時間**」、「**狀態**」、「**比較**」、「**讓步**」，要看前後句意決定，「文法寶典」p.533 有總整理。

as 表「**時間**」和「**狀態**」容易搞混，例如：

He did *as he was told*. (他按照指示做了。) ——表「狀態」
light〔laɪt〕*adj.* 輕淡的；不油膩的

6. *Unless you eat more now*, you will be hungry later.

unless 引導副詞子句，表「**否定條件**」，作「除非；如果不」解，是 *if…not* 的加強語氣，等於 *If* you do*n't* eat more now, you will be hungry later. (如果你現在不多吃點，你待會兒會餓。)

7. Let's go *if you're done*.

be done「做完某事」，吃完飯後或做完工作後，你可以説

I'm done. 或 *I'm finished.* 這是慣用語,文法上無法解釋,凡是表示「你已經完成你正在做的事」,都可以說 *I'm done.* 或 *I'm finished.* 等於 I've finished what I'm doing. 句中 if 子句表「**條件**」,修飾 go。再次強調,if 子句用現在式,主要子句不一定用 shall, will,**要把條件句的公式從腦海中除掉**。

8. *Now that we are here*, how about seeing a movie?

now that (既然),引導副詞子句,表「**原因**」,修飾動名詞 seeing。表「**原因**」的連接詞有很多,能用在這個句中的有 5 個:

Now that	
Seeing that	we are here, how about seeing
Considering that	a movie?
Since	既然
Because	因為 → 我們在這裡,看場電影如何?

how about 是 *how do you feel about* 的省略。

9. *Whatever movie you like*, it's fine with me.

複合關係代名詞 *whatever* 也可以當形容詞用,加上後面所修飾的字,和複合關代用法相同,Whatever movie 引導副詞子句,表「**讓步**」,在子句中,又做 like 的受詞,等於 *No matter what* movie。

TEST *13* 副詞子句

選出一個<u>最正確</u>的答案。

( ) 1. She studied French _____ she was in Paris.
    (A) during   (B) while   (C) if   (D) that

( ) 2. He has been here _____ he came to this room.
    (A) since   (B) from   (C) after (D) later

( ) 3. Let's wait _____ the next bus comes.
    (A) since   (B) until   (C) and   (D) for

( ) 4. He practices _____ he has a chance.
    (A) that   (B) how
    (C) whenever   (D) in

( ) 5. Although he is poor, _____ is honest.
    (A) but he   (B) so he   (C) and he (D) he

( ) 6. John is lying in bed, _____.
    (A) though he is tired
    (B) but he cannot fall asleep
    (C) because he is busy
    (D) as he at school

( ) 7. _____ I am sick, I have to see a doctor.
    (A) What   (B) How   (C) When (D) Which

( ) 8. _____ I meet him, what should I tell him?
    (A) Suppose (B) Only if (C) If only (D) Unless

( ) 9. I did not go to bed _____.
    (A) so I was asleep
    (B) because I was tired
    (C) when I was lying in bed
    (D) even though I was sleepy

( ) 10. He trembled _____ he spoke.
    (A) as   (B) although   (C) where (D) that

( ) 11. It will not be long _____ he appears.
    (A) so   (B) before   (C) if   (D) as

( ) 12. _____ comes, he will be welcome.
    (A) No matter whom   (B) No matter who
    (C) No matter that   (D) Whomever

( ) 13. Come _____ you like.
    (A) till   (B) since
    (C) whoever   (D) as often as

( ) 14. _____ as the book is, I don't like it at all.
    (A) Interesting   (B) Interested
    (C) Interest   (D) Interests

( ) 15. _____, the thief ran away.
    (A) No sooner had he seen the policeman
    (B) When seen the policeman
    (C) As soon as he saw the policeman
    (D) When the policeman seen him

【Answers】

1. **B** *while*（當…時候）引導副詞子句，修飾 studied。

2. **A** 自從他來到這個房間，就一直在這裡。
   since 前面用「現在完成式」，*since* 後用「過去式」。

3. **B** Let's wait *until the next bus comes*.
   我們等到下一部公車來。

4. **C** He practices *whenever he has a chance*.
   他一有機會就練習。
   whenever（無論何時）引導副詞子句。

5. **D** 英文和中文不一樣，前面有 *Although*，後面不可再接 *but*。

6. **B** 約翰躺在床上，但他睡不著。
   其他副詞子句的句意都不合理。

7. **C** *When* 引導副詞子句，修飾 have to see。

8. **A** *Suppose I meet him*, what should I tell him?
   如果我遇見他，我該跟他說什麼？
   $$\begin{cases} \textbf{\textit{Suppose}} \ (\textbf{\textit{that}}) \quad 如果 \\ = \textbf{\textit{Supposing}} \ (\textbf{\textit{that}}) \\ = \textbf{\textit{If}} \end{cases}$$

9. **D** I did not go to bed *even though I was sleepy*.
   即使我很睏，我也沒去睡覺。
   even though 即使（= *even if*）
   sleepy〔'slipɪ〕*adj.* 想睡的　　asleep〔ə'slip〕*adj.* 睡著的

10. **A** He trembled ***as*** *he spoke.* 當他說話時，他在發抖。
tremble (ˈtrɛmbḷ) *v.* 發抖

11. **B** ***not long before***··· 不久就···【詳見「文法寶典」p.495】

12. **B** ***No matter who*** *comes*, he will be welcome.
無論誰來，都歡迎。

> ***No matter who*** (無論是誰) 引導副詞子句，表讓步。
> = ***Whoever***

13. **D** Come ***as often as*** *you like.* 你什麼時候想來就來。

> ***as often as*** 無論何時；每次【詳見「文法寶典」p.494】
> = ***whenever***
> = ***each time***

14. **A** *Interesting* **as** *the book is*, I don't like it at all.

= ***Although*** *the book is interesting*, I don't like it at all.
interesting (有趣的)，修飾事物；interested (感興趣的)，
修飾人。as 在第二個字作「雖然」解。

15. **C** ***As soon as*** *he saw the policeman*, the thief ran away.
那小偷一看到警察就跑掉了。

= ***No sooner*** had he seen the policeman ***than*** the thief
ran away.

no sooner···than (一···就) 的用法，詳見「文法寶典」
p.496。

UNIT *14*

名詞子句（Noun Clause）

· ·

　　名詞子句和名詞一樣，可當主詞、受詞、補語、同位語等，引導名詞子句的連接詞有：*that*, *whether* （是否），*if*（是否），疑問代名詞（who, whose, whom, which, what），疑問副詞（when, where, why, how），和複合關係代名詞（what, whatever, whoever, whosever, whomever, whichever）。

　　這一回的劇情是，你和你的外國朋友吃完飯、看完電影後，你和他所說的話。

1. What you paid was too much.

Was it?

2. I promise that I will treat you next time.

Great!

3. The problem is that I'm short of cash.

I can help.

14. 名詞子句（Noun Clause）

What you paid was too much. 你付的太多了。

I promise *that* I will treat you next time. 我保證下次我請你。

The problem is *that* I'm short of cash. 問題是我現在缺錢。

【背誦技巧：別人請客後說】

I was wondering *if* you could give me a loan of one hundred dollars. 不知道你是否可以借我一百元。

Whether you agree *or not* doesn't matter. 你同意不同意都沒關係。

I'm afraid I must be going. 恐怕我得走了。

【一、二句相關】

I suggest *that* we meet again soon. 我建議我們很快再見面。

Please tell me *when* you are free. 請告訴我你何時有空。

Whoever runs away is a coward. 誰逃跑誰就是懦夫。

【一、二、三句相關連】

【文法解析】

1. *What you paid* was too much.
   <u>名詞子句</u>

   複合關代 **What** 引導名詞子句，做**主詞**，子句中的 What，做 paid 的受詞，相當於 *The money that*。

2. I promise *that I will treat you next time.*

   that 引導名詞子句，做 promise 的**受詞**，that 是純粹連接詞，沒有代名作用，that 子句做受詞時，that 可以省略。
   【比較】I promise *that* I will treat you next time. 【語氣正式】
   　　　　I promise I will treat you next time. 【語氣輕鬆，常用】
   　　　　treat〔trit〕*v.* 請客；招待

3. The problem is *that I'm short of cash.*

   that 引導名詞子句，做**主詞補語**，口語中 that 可省略，或用逗點代替，寫成：The problem is, I'm short of cash.
   be short of 缺乏　　cash〔kæʃ〕*n.* 現金

4. I was wondering *if you could give me a loan of one hundred dollars.*

   美國人要借錢時，習慣先說 **I was wondering**，表示客氣，wonder 是「不知道，但想知道」。if 子句做 wondering 的受詞，凡是表「詢問」或「懷疑」的句子，如 ask, see, try, wonder, doubt, know 等之後的 if，等於 whether，作「是否」解。　　loan〔lon〕*n.* 貸款；借款
   【比較】I was wondering if you could *give me a loan.*
   　　　　　　　　【誤，loan 後須接 of *sth.*】
   英文就這麼難，差一點就不行，背句子為上策。

5. *Whether* you agree *or not* doesn't matter.
　　　名詞子句

Whether…or not 引導名詞子句，做 doesn't matter 的**主詞**，or not 可以省略，說成：Whether you agree doesn't matter.

Whether…or not 也可引導副詞子句，如：

Whether you agree *or not*, it doesn't matter.
　　　副詞子句
【詳見「文法寶典」p.484】

6. I'm afraid *I must be going*.
　　　　名詞子句

I must be going 是名詞子句，連接詞 that 被省略，名詞子句做 I'm afraid (of) 的**受詞**，that 子句不能做介系詞的受詞，of 必須省略。

> 類似的形容詞有：sorry, glad, aware, surprised, delighted, disappointed 等，後面的 that 可以省略。
> 【詳見「文法寶典」p.480】

【比較】
I'm afraid that I must be going. 【正，少用】
I'm afraid I must be going. 【正，常用】
I'm afraid *of the fact that* I must be going.
　　【文法正確，但美國人不用】

7. I suggest *that we meet again soon.*

that 引導名詞子句，做 suggest 的**受詞**，由於 suggest 是慾望動詞，we 後省略了 should。傳統文法中，慾望動詞後的連接詞 that 不省略，但現在無論口語或是書寫英文中，that 都可以省略。

【比較】I suggest *that* we meet again soon. 【語氣正式】

I suggest we meet again soon. 【語氣輕鬆】

8. Please tell me *when you are free.*

疑問副詞 *when* 引導名詞子句，做 tell 的**直接受詞**。這句話也可說成：Please tell me <u>when you will be free</u>.

名詞子句

Are you free?、Are you busy?、Are you available? 等句子，常用現在式代替未來式。【詳見「一口氣背會話」p.133】也可以把 when you are free 看成副詞子句。

Please tell me *when you are free.*

= When you are free, please tell me.

在這裡無論 when 子句當名詞或副詞，句意相同。

9. *Whoever runs away* is a coward.

名詞子句

複合關代 *Whoever* 引導名詞子句，做 is 的**主詞**，在名詞子句中，Whoever 做 runs 的主詞，等於 Anyone who。

coward〔ˋkauɚd〕*n.* 膽小鬼；懦夫

UNIT 13~16

TEST *14* 名詞子句

選出一個<u>最正確</u>的答案。

( ) 1. I wonder _____ my brother has been here.
(A) that (B) which (C) if (D) though

( ) 2. We don't know _____ this is a true story or not.
(A) whether (B) that
(C) which (D) what

( ) 3. It is true _____ a lot of novels are not worth reading.
(A) what (B) that (C) which (D) where

( ) 4. I cannot accept the fact _____ he is dead.
(A) if (B) that (C) why (D) which

( ) 5. He said _____ nothing would make him change his mind.
(A) which (B) why (C) that (D) nor

( ) 6. Nobody knows _____ she would do such a stupid thing.
(A) how (B) why (C) which (D) than

( ) 7. You may do _____ you like.
(A) anything what (B) whatever
(C) anyhow (D) which

( ) 8. I don't doubt _____ you will win.
(A) if (B) whenever (C) that (D) when

UNIT 13~16

( ) 9. Few people know _____.
    (A) how hard he works
    (B) how to do
    (C) how hard does he work
    (D) how he works hard

( ) 10. You may give this pen to _____ wants it.
    (A) whomever   (B) whosever
    (C) whoever   (D) anyone

( ) 11. I asked her _____ was the matter.
    (A) if   (B) whether
    (C) anything   (D) what

( ) 12. Tell me _____ you have read recently.
    (A) what books   (B) what do
    (C) which books do   (D) any books

( ) 13. _____ we need it is a different matter.
    (A) If   (B) Whether
    (C) That   (D) What

( ) 14. He accused me _____.
    (A) that I copied   (B) of that I copied
    (C) of copying   (D) copying

( ) 15. I _____ you've heard about my situation.
    (A) take it that   (B) take that
    (C) take   (D) don't take

【Answers】

1. **C**　我不知道我弟弟是否已經在這裡。
　　wonder（不知道；想知道），*ask*（問），*doubt*（懷疑）後
　　的名詞子句用 *whether* 或 *if* 來引導。

2. **A**　don't know 後用 *whether* 或 *if* 引導名詞子句。

3. **B**　的確，很多小說不值得一讀。
　　that 引導名詞子句，做這句話的真正主詞，*It* 是虛主詞。
　　It is true that 的確　　novel〔ˈnɑvl̩〕*n.* 小說
　　worth〔wɝθ〕*adj.* 值得的

4. **B**　*that* 引導名詞子句，做 the fact 的同位語。

5. **C**　*that* 引導名詞子句，做 said 的受詞。

6. **B**　沒有人知道，她為何會做這麼愚蠢的事。
　　依句意，*why* 引導名詞子句，做 knows 的受詞。

7. **B**　You may do **_whatever_ you like**.　你喜歡做什麼就做什麼。
　　　　　　　　　　　名詞子句
　　= You may do anything *that you like*.
　　複合關代 *whatever* 引導名詞子句，做 do 的受詞，在子句
　　中，*whatever* 做 like 的受詞，此時，*whatever* 是 what
　　的加強語氣。

8. **C**　*do not doubt*（= *believe*）後面須接 *that* 子句做受詞。
　　【詳見「文法寶典」p.481】

9. **A** 疑問副詞 *when*，*where*，*why*，*how* 都可引導名詞子句，
how 在本句中，除了當連接詞用，還修飾 hard。**名詞子句**
要用敘述句形式，不可用疑問句形式。

10. **C** You may give this pen to ___*whoever* wants it___.

名詞子句

whoever 引導名詞子句，做 to 的受詞，在子句中，
whoever 做 wants 的主詞，所以用主格。

11. **D** *what* 引導名詞子句，做 asked 的直接受詞，在該子句中，
what 做 be 動詞的主詞。
what was the matter 怎麼了（= *what was wrong*）

12. **A** 告訴我你最近讀了什麼書。

Tell me ___*what books*___ you have read recently.
‖
what
what 在此是疑問形容詞，加上所修飾的字，和疑問代名詞
一樣，引導名詞子句，做 Tell 的直接受詞。
recently（'risṇtlɪ）*adv.* 最近

13. **B** 我們是否需要，是另一回事。
Whether 引導名詞子句，做 is 的主詞。If 子句不能做主
詞。　　　matter（'mætɚ）*n.* 事情

14. **C** ***accuse sb. of sth.*** 控告某人某事【不能省略 of，接 that 子句】
He accused me that I copied his book.（誤）
He accused me of the fact that I copied his book.（誤）

15. **A** ***that* 子句不可做 *admire*（稱讚），*allow*（允許），*love*（愛），**
***like*（喜歡），*take*（認為）等的受詞。**【詳見「文法寶典」p.482】
I take it that⋯「我認為⋯」，that 子句做 it 的同位語。

UNIT *15*

形容詞子句（Adjective Clause）

‧‧‧‧‧‧‧‧‧‧‧‧‧‧‧‧‧‧‧‧‧‧‧‧‧‧‧‧‧‧‧‧

　　形容詞子句通常用來修飾名詞，連接詞有關係代
名詞（who, whose, whom, which, of which, that）、
準關係代名詞（as, but, than）、關係副詞（when,
where, why, how）。

 你是主角，和外國人去郊外拜訪朋友

15. 形容詞子句 (Adjective Clause)

Sunday is the day *when* I am least busy.	星期天我最不忙。
I usually go to the village, *where* I can enjoy some fresh air.	我通常到村莊裡享受一點新鮮空氣。
This is the reason *why* you can't reach me.	這就是為什麼你連絡不到我的原因。

【背誦技巧：when, where, why, how 引導形容詞子句】

This is *how* I stay in shape.	這是我保持健康的方法。
John is the man *who* goes hiking with me.	約翰就是和我去爬山的人。
The house *whose* roof we see is his home.	我們看到屋頂的那棟房子就是他家。

【who, whose 引導形容詞子句】

The dog *which* is barking belongs to him.	正在叫的那隻狗是他的。
John's daughter is the most beautiful girl *I have ever seen.*	約翰的女兒是我見過最美麗的女孩。
She gave us a warm welcome, *as* was usual with her.	她熱情地歡迎我們，她通常如此。

【who 完了就是 which】

UNIT 13～16

【文法解析】

1. Sunday is the day *when I am least busy.*

   關係副詞 *when* 引導形容詞子句，修飾 the day。這句話可簡化為：Sunday is when I am least busy.
   little 的比較級是 less（較小；較少），最高級是 least（最不；最少）。

2. I usually go to the village, *where I can enjoy some fresh air.*

   關係副詞 *where* 引導形容詞子句，修飾 the village。
   village〔'vɪlɪdʒ〕*n.* 村莊

3. This is the reason *why you can't reach me.*

   關係副詞 *why* 引導形容詞子句，修飾 the reason，這句話可以簡化為：This is why you can't reach me.
   reach〔ritʃ〕*v.* 聯絡；到達

4. This is *how I stay in shape.*

   這句話源自：This is the way *how I stay in shape.*（不用）

   還可以說成：This is the way *I stay in shape.*
   stay in shape 保持健康

5. John is the man *who goes hiking with me.*

   關代 *who* 引導形容詞子句，修飾 the man，who 在子句中代替 the man，做 goes 的主詞。
   【比較】***go hiking*** 去爬山（走上去）；去健行；徒步旅行
   　　　　go mountain climbing 去登山（爬上去）

Let's go hiking in the countryside.

（我們到鄉下走走。）

Let's go hiking on Yangmingshan.

（我們去陽明山爬山。）

countryside〔'kʌntrɪ,saɪd〕*n.* 鄉間；鄉村地區

6. The house *whose roof we see* is his home.

關代 *whose* 是 who 的所有格，可代替人及非人，whose roof 引導形容詞子句，修飾 the house，在子句中，whose roof 做 see 的受詞。　　roof〔ruf〕*n.* 屋頂

7. The dog *which is barking* belongs to him.

關代 *which* 引導形容詞子句，修飾 The dog，which 在子句中代替 The dog，做 is 的主詞。　　bark〔bɑrk〕*v.* 吠叫

8. John's daughter is the most beautiful girl *(that) I have ever seen.*

關代 *that* 引導形容詞子句，修飾 girl。先行詞前有最高級形容詞時，關代通常用 that，因為在子句中做 seen 的受詞，常省略。【詳見「文法寶典」p.153】

9. She gave us a warm welcome, *as was usual with her.*

as 是準關代，引導形容詞子句，修飾前面整句話。
把 *as is usual with sb.*（某人通常如此），*as is often the case*（是常有的事），*as is natural*（是自然的事）當成慣用語來背，as 後沒有主詞，所以做準關代。【詳見「文法寶典」p.160, p.499】

UNIT 13~16

TEST *15* 形容詞子句

選出一個<u>最正確</u>的答案。

(   ) 1. I wish to read a book _____ is both easy and interesting.
        (A) why   (B) how   (C) when   (D) which

(   ) 2. I'll never forget the day _____ Mrs. Smith left us.
        (A) why   (B) when   (C) how   (D) where

(   ) 3. That is the reason _____ people laugh at him.
        (A) which   (B) what   (C) why   (D) how

(   ) 4. They want to sell the house _____ has only one door.
        (A) where   (B) which   (C) there   (D) it

(   ) 5. The house _____ we live is beautiful.
        (A) that   (B) which   (C) where   (D) what

(   ) 6. This is the house _____ which I was born.
        (A) in   (B) for   (C) at   (D) on

(   ) 7. He hid the money _____ his wife couldn't find it.
        (A) where   (B) which   (C) there   (D) in which

(　) 8. He tried to escape, _____ he found impossible.
　　(A) which　(B) that　(C) as　(D) when

(　) 9. It was raining hard, _____ kept us indoors.
　　(A) that　(B) which　(C) as　(D) where

(　) 10. This is the man _____ is honest.
　　(A) who I believe　(B) whom I believe
　　(C) believes　(D) believed

(　) 11. The books _____ pictures in them are interesting.
　　(A) which has　(B) with which
　　(C) which having　(D) which have

(　) 12. I don't like the man to _____ he is speaking.
　　(A) that　(B) who　(C) whom　(D) which

(　) 13. I met Mary, _____ told me the news.
　　(A) that　(B) who　(C) which　(D) she

(　) 14. Do you see the bus _____ windows have been broken?
　　(A) which　(B) whose　(C) its　(D) where

(　) 15. He is as brave a solider _____ ever lived.
　　(A) as　(B) who　(C) that　(D) what

UNIT 13~16

【Answers】

1. **D** 關係代名詞 **which** 引導形容詞子句，修飾 book，這裡的 which 可用 that 代替。

2. **B** 關係副詞 **when**，**where**，**why**，**how** 可引導形容詞子句，根據句意，表「時間」用 **when**。

3. **C** This is the reason **why** *people laugh at him.*
   表「原因」，關係副詞用 **why**。　　**laugh at** 嘲笑

4. **B** 關係代名詞 **which** 引導形容詞子句，在子句中，做 has 的主詞。(A) where 無代名作用。

5. **C** The house **where** *we live* is beautiful. 【最常用】
   = The house **in which** *we live* is beautiful. 【常用】
   = The house **which** *we live in* is beautiful. 【少用】
   關係副詞 **where** 無代名作用；關代 **which** 有代名作用。

6. **A** in which = where

7. **A** hide〔haɪd〕v. 隱藏【三態變化：hide-hid-hid/hidden】
   這句話源自：He hid the money *in a place* where his wife couldn't find it. 句中的 *in a place* 省略後，變成副詞子句：
   He hid the money **where** *his wife couldn't find it.*
   他把錢藏在他太太找不到的地方。

8. **A** 他想要逃走，這件事他覺得不可能。
   He tried to escape, **which** *he found impossible.*
   關係代名詞 **which** 引導形容詞子句，修飾前面的不定詞片語 to escape，在子句中，**which** 又做 found 的受詞。前有逗點，不可用 that。

9. **B** It was raining hard, ***which** kept us indoors.*
　　　　主要子句

關代 ***which*** 引導形容詞子句，修飾前面整句話，***which*** 前
有逗點，是補述用法的形容詞子句，關代不可用 *that*。
【詳見「文法寶典」p.162】
rain hard 下大雨　　indoors〔ˋɪnˋdorz〕*adv.* 在室內

10. **A** This is the man ***who*** I believe *is honest.*
　　　　　　　　　　　　　　　　　　插入

關代 ***who*** 引導形容詞子句，修飾 the man，在子句中做 is
的主詞，所以用主格 ***who***，子句中的 I believe 是插入語。
插入語的動詞常是：***believe***，***imagine***，***guess***，***suppose***，
say 等。【詳見「文法寶典」p.163, p.651】

11. **D** 裡面有圖畫的書很有趣。　　關代 ***which*** 引導形容詞子句，
修飾 The books，在子句中，做 have 的主詞。

12. **C** I don't like the man *to **whom** he is speaking.*
我不喜歡正在和他說話的人。
關代 ***whom*** 引導形容詞子句，修飾 the man，在子句中，
做 to 的受詞，所以是受格 ***whom***。這句話也可說成：I
don't like the man *he is speaking to.* 或 I don't like the
man ***that** he is speaking to.* 但現代美語中，美國人不說：
I don't like the man whom he is speaking to.（誤）

13. **B** 這句話是補述用法的形容詞子句，對前面的話加以補充說
明，關代不可用 that。【參照第 9 題】

14. **B** 關代所有格 ***whose*** 引導形容詞子句，修飾 the bus，在
子句中，***whose*** 是 windows 的所有格。

15. **A** 他是有史以來最英勇的軍人。　　先行詞前有 ***as, the same,***
such 時，關代用 ***as***，as 被稱為準關代。【詳見「文法寶典」p.159】
brave〔brev〕*adj.* 勇敢的　　soldier〔ˋsoldʒɚ〕*n.* 軍人

UNIT *16*

片 語（Phrase）

● ●

　　二個以上的字就稱爲片語，用途和子句一樣，主要可當名詞、形容詞、副詞用，結構上來分，主要有動詞片語、不定詞片語、分詞片語、動名詞片語、介系詞片語。

　　美國人喜歡談美女，這一回你是主角，談論某位漂亮女孩。

4. She treated us with kindness.

She did.

5. She is too young to get married.

I think you're right.

6. She is fond of learning.

So am I.

7. Mary wishes to go abroad for further studies.

That's a solid plan.

8. I like her attitude as well as her humor.

Me too.

9. She will succeed by means of hard work.

We all will.

16. 片 語（Phrase）

Mary *takes after* her mother.	瑪麗很像她媽媽。
They love *each other*.	她們深愛著彼此。
Mary is *all smiles*.	瑪麗滿臉笑容。

【背誦技巧：長得像，愛，微笑】

She treated us *with kindness*.	她對我們很好。
She is *too* young *to get married*.	她太年輕了，還不能結婚。
She *is fond of* learning.	她喜歡學習。

【年紀輕，喜歡學習】

Mary wishes *to go abroad for further studies*.	瑪麗希望出國留學。
I like her attitude *as well as* her humor.	我喜歡她的態度和她的幽默。
She will succeed *by means of* hard work.	藉由努力她會成功的。

【希望出國，我喜歡她】

【文法解析】

1. Mary *takes after* her mother.

 take after 是動詞片語，表「長得像」。

 Mary
 {
   takes after
   looks like
   resembles
   has a resemblance to
   bears a resemblance to
 }
 her mother.
 （瑪麗長得像她媽媽。）

 bear〔bɛr〕*v.* 有　　resemble〔rɪ'zɛmbḷ〕*v.* 像
 resemblance〔rɪ'zɛmbləns〕*n.* 相似；相似之處

2. They love *each other*.

 each other 是代名詞片語，做 love 的受詞，*each other* 和 *one another* 現在可以混用，但是 each other 強調「各個之間」的彼此，one another 強調「全體之間」的彼此，例如：

 My parents love
 {
   each other.
   one another.
 }
 （我父母親彼此相愛。）

 The three men distrusted
 {
   each other.
   one another.
 }

 （這三個人互相不信任。）

 英文中只有二個代名詞片語 *each other* 和 *one another*，只能做受詞，不能做主詞。

3. Mary is *all smiles*.

 all smiles 從結構上來分，是**名詞片語**，從功用上來分，是**形容詞片語**，也就是**名詞片語當形容詞片語用**。

be all smiles 滿臉笑容	be all eyes 專心看
be all ears 專心聽	
be all thumbs 笨手笨腳【手指全部都是大姆指，就不靈活了】	

4. She treated us *with kindness*.

with kindness 是介詞片語，當副詞片語用，修飾 treated，等於 kindly。這句話也可說成：She treated us well.

5. She is *too* young *to get married*.

to get married 是不定詞片語，當副詞片語用，修飾相關副詞 too。　　*too…to* 太…以致於不

6. She *is fond of* learning.

be fond of（喜歡）是動詞片語，等於 like。

She $\begin{cases} \textit{is fond of} \\ \text{likes} \\ \text{loves} \\ \text{enjoys} \end{cases}$ learning.（她喜歡學習。）

7. Mary wishes *to go abroad for further studies*.

不定詞片語 to go abroad for further studies 當名詞片語用，做 wishes 的受詞，在該片語中，for further studies 是介詞片語，當副詞片語用，修飾 go。

further〔ˈfɝðɚ〕*adj.* 更多的；進一步的

8. I like her attitude *as well as* her humor.

as well as 是對等連接詞片語，連接二個名詞片語 her attitude 和 her humor。as well as 連接二個主詞時，重點在前者，動詞與前面主詞一致，例如：*The teacher as well as* the students *is* expected to study hard.（老師和學生一樣應該用功讀書。）

9. She will succeed *by means of* hard work.

片語介系詞

by means of「藉由；靠著」，在此等於 through、with，或 *by*。**片語介系詞**的功用相當於**介系詞**。介系詞片語通常是「介詞＋名詞」，常當形容詞或副詞用。

TEST *16* 片語

選出一個最<u>正確</u>的答案。

( ) 1. To master a foreign language _____ not easy.
    (A) is   (B) are
    (C) has   (D) were

( ) 2. We ought to help _____.
    (A) to each other   (B) to one another
    (C) with one another   (D) each other

( ) 3. This book is _____.
    (A) worthy being read   (B) great value
    (C) of great value   (D) with great value

( ) 4. John _____ his father both in looks and in character.
    (A) likes   (B) takes after
    (C) like   (D) looks after

( ) 5. John went _____.
    (A) to the library every night last week
    (B) every night to the library last week
    (C) last week every night to the library
    (D) every night last week to the library

(   ) 6. Betty got up early _____ catching the first train.
    (A) to   (B) with the eye to
    (C) for   (D) with a view to

(   ) 7. You may call this number _____ I am not home.
    (A) in case   (B) with case
    (C) in this case   (D) in case of

(   ) 8. _____, are you all right?
    (A) Well done   (B) Nice job
    (C) Oh, my God   (D) Nice work

(   ) 9. Painting beautiful pictures _____ interesting work.
    (A) are   (B) were   (C) has   (D) is

(   ) 10. I _____ for you about twenty minutes.
    (A) have waiting   (B) have been waiting
    (C) am waiting   (D) will been waiting

(   ) 11. He is a famous writer _____ all over the world.
    (A) knowing   (B) knew
    (C) knows   (D) known

(　) 12. I have a taxi waiting for us _____.
      (A) at the door   (B) in front of door
      (C) out of front   (D) before door

(　) 13. Please stay _____.
      (A) till after dinner   (B) after till dinner
      (C) from dinner on   (D) before till dinner

(　) 14. The invention of the smartphone _____ the world.
      (A) change   (B) to change
      (C) has changed
      (D) will have been changed

(　) 15. The girl _____ was very cute.
      (A) played the piano   (B) to play the piano
      (C) plays the piano   (D) playing the piano

UNIT 13～16

【Answers】

1. **A** 不定詞片語 To master a foreign language 當名詞用，做主詞，動詞用單數，敘述事實用現在式。

2. **D** *each other* 和 *one another* 是代名詞片語，做 help 的受詞。

3. **C** of + 抽象 N. = 形容詞片語
of great value = very valuable 【詳見「文法寶典」p.588】
(A) 應改成 worth reading 或 worthy of being read。

4. **B** *take after*「像」，是**動詞片語**，等於 *look like*。
約翰在外表和個性都像他父親。
looks〔luks〕*n. pl.* 外表；樣子
character〔ˈkærɪktɚ〕*n.* 個性

5. **A** 有兩個以上副詞修飾語時，正常順序為：地點、狀態、
次數、時間。

John went <u>to the library</u> <u>every night</u> <u>last week</u>.
　　　　　地點　　　　　次數　　　　時間

6. **D** *with a view to*（目的是為了）是**片語介系詞**，用法相當於
介系詞，等於 *with an eye to*。【詳見「文法寶典」p.514】
(C) for + V-ing 不可表「目的」，for + N. 表「目的」。
Betty got up early *for* the first train.【正】
（貝蒂早起是為了趕第一班火車。）

7. **A** *in case* 是**片語連接詞**，相當於 *if*。【詳見「文法寶典」p.21, 520】
in this case 在這種情況下
in case of 如果；萬一【要接名詞】

8. **C** Oh, my God（噢，天啊）是**感嘆詞片語**，獨立存在。
(A) Well done. 做得好。(= *Nice work.* = *Nice job.*)

9. **D** **動名詞片語**和不定詞片語一樣，當主詞時，動詞用單數。

10. **B** I <u>have been waiting</u> *for you about twenty minutes*.
　　　動詞片語
「現在完成進行式」可用來加強「現在完成式」的語氣。

11. **D**　He is a famous writer *known all over the world.*

分詞片語

分詞片語中，現在分詞表主動，過去分詞表被動，當形容詞用。

12. **A**　I have a taxi *waiting for us at the door.*

at the door 是介系詞片語，當副詞片語用，修飾 waiting。

(B) → out in front of the door

(C) → out front

> 「在門口」不能說成 *before the door*（誤），可以說成：at the door 或 out in front of the door，最常用的是 out front。【詳見「一口氣背會話」p.1237】

13. **A**　Please stay *till after dinner.* 請留到晚餐之後。

> 「介系詞＋介系詞」又稱「雙重介系詞」，常見的有：*from among*，*from behind*，*from under*，*till after*，*in between*…等。【詳見「文法寶典」p.544】

名詞片語當完全主詞

14. **C**　The <u>invention</u> of the smartphone ***has changed*** the world.

核心主詞　　　　　　　　　　　　　　　動詞片語

根據句意，用「現在完成式」。

smartphone〔'smɑrt,fon〕*n.* 智慧型手機

15. **D**　playing the piano 是分詞片語，當形容詞用。

The girl *playing the piano* was very cute.

= The girl *who played the piano* was very cute.

UNIT 13～16

UNIT *17*

倒裝、插入、省略

• •

　　有些句子為了加強語氣而倒裝，最常見的是，否定副詞放句首，助動詞或 be 動詞和主詞倒裝。有些句子為了避免重覆或簡化而省略，如 Thank you. 是 I thank you. 的省略，如果不知道這項省略，你會以為 Thank you. 是命令句。有些句子則為了補充說明而插入。

 這一回你是主角，和外國朋友談論風景，想起父親，也想到家。

1. What a beautiful day! You're right!

2. Never have I seen such a nice view. It's amazing!

3. I seldom, if ever, saw such a fine sight. I agree.

It's amazing!　真棒！

Wow〔wau〕哇！　　I see. 我明白。

Home is where the heart is. 家是心之所在。
It sure is. 的確是。

17. 倒裝、插入、省略

What a beautiful day!

Never have I seen such a nice view.

I *seldom*, *if ever*, saw such a fine sight.

【背誦技巧：二、三句意思相同】

多麼好的天氣！

我從來沒看過這麼好的景色。

即使有的話，我也很少看過這麼好的景色。

Not until now *did I* know it is so wonderful.

Happy is the man who is content.

What I am today I owe to my father.

【看到風景好，心裡快樂，想要感謝】

我現在才知道，這裡景色這麼棒。

【諺】知足常樂。

我今天的成就要歸功於我的父親。

Oh, *that* he could be with us!

Be it ever so humble, there is no place like home.

East or west, home is best.

【第一句承接上段，二、三句提到 home】

我多麼希望他能和我們在一起！

【諺】在家千日好，出門事事難。

【諺】東奔西跑，不如家裡最好。

【文法解析】

1. What a beautiful day! 【省略 it is】

   句子有敘述句、疑問句、命令句、感嘆句、祈願句、句尾
   附加句等六種。

   What 和 How 常引導感嘆句，組成方式為：

   ```
   What  ┐
         ├ ＋ 所修飾字 ＋ 主詞 ＋ 動詞！
   How   ┘
   ```

   主詞和動詞句意明確時常省略。

   【比較】What a beautiful day! 【正，常用】
   　　　　What a beautiful day it is! 【文法對，但美國人不說】
   　　　　【詳見「文法寶典」p.4, p.148, p.646】

2. *Never have I* seen such a nice view.

   否定副詞放在句首時，助動詞要放在主詞前面，形成倒裝。

   ```
   否定詞 ＋ ┌ 助動詞  ┐ ＋ 主詞…
            └ be 動詞 ┘
   ```

   這句話也可說成：I have *never* seen such a nice view.
   【詳見「文法寶典」p.629】

3. I *seldom*, *if ever*, saw such a fine sight.

   句子有時會在中間或尾部插入其他單字、片語，或子句。
   這句話也可說成：I seldom saw such a fine sight,
   if I *ever* saw one.。*if ever*，*if possible*，*if any* 等副詞子
   句插入，通常省略主詞和動詞。【詳見「文法寶典」p.653】
   可以把 *seldom*, *if ever*, 看成片語，運用在會話中，如：

I *seldom*, *if ever*, smoke. (我很少抽煙。)

I *seldom*, *if ever*, go camping. (我很少去露營。)

She *seldom*, *if ever*, goes on a date. (她很少去約會。)

seldom, *if ever*, 和 seldom 一樣，可以翻成「很少；幾乎不」。

4. *Not until* now *did I* know it is so wonderful.

= I didn't know it is so wonderful *until now*.

not…until~　直到~才…，Not until now 放在句首，助動詞 did 要放在主詞 I 前面，倒裝的目的在加強語氣。not until 的句型變化，詳見「文法寶典」p.492。

可以把「*Not until now did I know* + 句子」看成一個公式，指「我現在才知道」，如：

Not until now did I know you are rich.

（ 我現在才知道你很有錢。 ）

Not until now did I know I was set up.

（ 我現在才知道我被陷害。 ）

5. *Happy is* the man *who is content*.

這句話原來是 The man *who is content* is happy.，完全主詞太長，核心主詞 man 和動詞 is 太遠，為了加強語氣，強調主詞補語而倒裝。【詳見「文法寶典」p.637】

content 和 contented 都作「知足的」解，等於 satisfied，但 contented 較少用。

6. *What I am today* I owe to my father.
　　　　受　詞

= I owe *what I am today* to my father.
　　　　　　　受　詞

受詞放在句首的倒裝，是為了強調受詞。【詳見「文法寶典」p.635】

7. *Oh*, *that* he could be with us!

*O*h, *that* 是 *Oh*, *how I wish that* 的省略，詳見「文法寶典」p.646 和 p.370。這句話也可説成：I wish he could be with us!

8. *Be it ever so humble*, there is no place like home.

這句話是 Let it be ever so humble，…的省略，也可以説成：No matter how humble (*it may be*), ….。【詳見「文法寶典」p.530】

這句話字面意思是「無論家多麼簡陋，沒有地方像家一樣好。」，引申為「在家千日好，出門事事難。」

ever so 非常地 (= *very*)

humble〔ˈhʌmbl̩〕*adj.* 謙虛的；卑微的；簡陋的

9. *East or west*, home is best.【省略 the】

這句話源自 Whether you go east or west, home is (the) best. 中國人説「東西南北」，美國人説「北南東西」north, south, east, or west，幸好「東西」和中文相同。通常形容詞最高級要加 the，如：Home is *the best* place to relax. (家是放鬆最好的地方。) 但此句例外，為了前後二句音節相同，而省略 the。*home is best* 已經變成慣用語。再一次證明，英文文法規則是研究不完的，背短句是最簡單的方法。背過的句子説出來、寫出來最有信心。

有些美國人喜歡幽默地説：North, south, east, or west, you are the best. (走遍東西南北，你最棒。)【這句有 the】

TEST *17* 倒裝、插入、省略

選出一個<u>最正確</u>的答案。

( ) 1. _____ he is!
   (A) What a clever man (B) How a clever man
   (C) What clever a man (D) What clever

( ) 2. Not only _____, but he saw her.
   (A) did he come   (B) he came
   (C) came he   (D) he comes

( ) 3. Hardly _____ started when I heard a man
   call my name.
   (A) did the car   (B) had the car
   (C) the car had   (D) the car did

( ) 4. I have never been to the U.S., _____.
   (A) nor he has   (B) so has he
   (C) nor does he   (D) nor has he

( ) 5. He is going home _____ is she.
   (A) and neither   (B) but neither
   (C) and so   (D) so neither

( ) 6. _____ this would come true.
   (A) Little I dreamed   (B) Little did I dreamed
   (C) Little did I dream   (D) Little do I dream

(　) 7. Only when you are away from home _____.
    (A) will you realize how sweet home is
    (B) you will miss your parents
    (C) you know your parents do love you
    (D) then you want to write letters home

(　) 8. Not for a moment _____ the truth of your story.
    (A) he has doubted   (B) he doubts
    (C) he did doubt   (D) did he doubt

(　) 9. This is, _____, a great piece of news.
    (A) I wonder   (B) indeed
    (C) if possible   (D) if any

(　) 10. Do not use your cell phone while _____.
    (A) walking   (B) you were walking
    (C) walk   (D) you walks

(　) 11. When _____ his opinion, he remained silent.
    (A) asking   (B) asked
    (C) he is asked   (D) he is asking

(　) 12. _____ a poor farmer and his wife.
    (A) Lived there once
    (B) Once lived there
    (C) There once lived   (D) Lived once

UNIT 17 ~ 20

(   ) 13. The man _____ would win lost the game.

        (A) who I thought

        (B) I thought who

        (C) who thought I

        (D) whom I thought

(   ) 14. _____ that young man is?

        (A) Do you think who

        (B) Who do you think

        (C) Who you think

        (D) You think who

(   ) 15. Not until I lay in bed _____ of the people.

        (A) did I think   (B) I did think

        (C) do I think   (D) so I think

【Answers】

1. **A** 感嘆句的組成：$\begin{Bmatrix} What \\ How \end{Bmatrix}$ + 所修飾字 + 主詞 + 動詞！

    【詳見「文法寶典」p.4】

    (B) → How clever a man

2. **A** *Not only* 放在句首，助動詞須放在主詞前**倒裝**。

    【詳見「文法寶典」p.629】

3. **B** *Hardly* (幾乎不)、*Scarcely* (幾乎不) 放在句首，助動詞須放在主詞前**倒裝**。

*Hardly **had** the car **started when** I **heard** a man call my name.*

= The car **had** *hardly* **started when** I **heard** a man call me.

（車子一發動，我就聽到有個男人在叫我。）

過去先發生，用「過去完成式」，後發生用「過去簡單式」。用否定副詞 Hardly（幾乎不）把前後時間擺平，所以 **hardly…when** 作「一…就～」解。

4. **D** **nor has he** 源自 **nor has he** been to the U.S.。nor、neither 放在句首時，主詞與助動詞須**倒裝**，作「也不；也沒有」解，事實上它是個省略句。【詳見「文法寶典」p.643】

5. **C** **and so is she** 源自 **and so is she** going home。**so** 用於肯定句，表示「也」，需要**倒裝**。【詳見「文法寶典」p.643】

6. **C** __Little__ *did* I *dream* this would come true.
　　副詞

（我一點都沒想到這會成真。）

little 正常情況是形容詞，當副詞時，等於 *not…at all*（一點也不）。否定副詞 *Little* 放在句首，助動詞須放在主詞前**倒裝**。

7. **A** **Only** + 副詞（片語、子句）+ **助動詞** + **主詞**

唯有當你離開家的時候，才知道家的甜美。

8. **D** *Not for a moment did* he *doubt* the truth of your story.

（他從未懷疑你故事的眞實性。）

否定副詞片語 *Not for a moment* 放在句首，助動詞須放在主詞前面**倒裝**。

not for a moment 從未（= *never*）

9. **B** 副詞 *indeed*（的確）是插入語。【詳見「文法寶典」p.656】

10. **A** Do not use your cell phone *while* (*you are*) *walking.*

when, *while*, *if*, *though*, *as* 等引導副詞子句，句意明確時，可省略主詞和 be 動詞。【詳見「文法寶典」p.645】

11. **B** *When* (*he was*) *asked his opinion*, he remained silent.

（當被問到他的意見時，他保持沈默。）

12. **C** There is, There are 的變化型有：There live, There come 等。【詳見「文法寶典」p.250】

句中 There once lived… = Once there lived…

這句話的意思是「從前有一位貧窮的農夫和他的妻子。」

在此 live 作「存在」解，不作「居住」解。

once〔wʌns〕*adv.* 曾經；從前；有一次

【比較】A poor farmer and his wife *once* lived there.

（有一位貧窮的農夫和他的太太曾經住在那裡。）

13. **A**　The man ***who*** *I thought* would win lost the game.
　　　　　　　　插入語

（我以為會贏的那個人卻輸了比賽。）

關係代名詞和動詞之間往往有插入語，插入語的動詞

通常是：believe, imagine, guess, suppose, say 等。

【詳見「文法寶典」p.163, 651】

　　　　　　　　名詞子句

14. **B**　| *Who* | **do you think** | *that young man is* | ?

（你認為那個年輕人是誰？）

疑問詞 + **do you think**（believe, imagine, guess, say,

suppose…）所形成的疑問句中，是將名詞子句的疑問詞

放在句首，而 do you think 是主要子句，而不是插入語。

【詳見「文法寶典」p.147, 405, 406, 652】

【比較】*Do you think who that young man is?*【誤，句意不清】

　　　　你不能問人家說：「你認為那個年輕人是誰了嗎？」

　　　　Do you know who that young man is?【正】

　　　　（你知道那個年輕人是誰嗎？）

15. **A**　***Not until*** *I lay in bed* did I think of the people.

= I didn't think of the people ***until*** *I lay in bed.*

（直到我躺在床上，我才想到那些人。）

not…until　直到…才

Not until 放在句首，助動詞要放在主詞前面。

【詳見「文法寶典」p.492，not…until 的句型變化】

UNIT 18

主詞與動詞的一致

· ·

Twenty days 當主詞，動詞用單數還是複數呢？A number of 和 The number of 的區別為何？有時主詞是複數，動詞用單數，有時主詞是單數，動詞卻是複數，臨時造句很危險，背句子學文法最安全。

 你是主角，和外國人閒聊。

Mine too. 來自 Most of my time is…, too.

That's odd. 很奇怪。　　Indeed. 的確。

18. 主詞與動詞的一致

Twenty days *seems* a long time to wait.

等二十天似乎是相當長的時間。

Twenty days *have* passed since I last saw him.

自從我上次見到他已經二十天了。

Most of my time *is* spent in studying.

我大部分的時間都花在讀書上。

【背誦技巧：前二句都有 Twenty days，第三句等待的時間在讀書】

A number of students *are* absent today.

今天有好幾位學生缺席。

There *is* a man and a woman at the door.

有一男一女在門口。

Every man, woman, and child here *is* happy.

這裡的每個男人、女人和小孩都很高興。

【幾個學生缺席，但門口有人】

Neither the students nor the teacher *wants* the party to be cancelled.

學生們和老師都不希望派對被取消。

Not you but I *am* in charge.

負責的不是你而是我。

Any of your friends *are* welcome to join us.

歡迎你的任何朋友加入我們。

【開派對，我負責，邀請你的朋友】

【文法解析】

1. <u>Twenty days</u> *seems* a long time *to wait*.
　　　主　詞

複數名詞如果表示「**一段時間**」、「**一筆金錢**」、「**一段距離**」、「**一個重量**」等，雖然形式上是複數，但意義上是單數時，動詞用單數。這裡的 Twenty days seems...，

等於 The number of twenty days seems...，表示二十天這段時間。

2. <u>Twenty days</u> *have* passed *since I last saw him*.
　　　主　詞

這句話的主詞 Twenty days 雖然是時間，但不表示「一段時間」，而表示二十天一天一天過去，**意義是複數，動詞也用複數**。

3. Most *of my time is* spent in studying.

most（大部分）		
all（全部）		
half（一半）		
the rest（其餘的）		
part（一部分）	of +	單數名詞 ＋ 單數動詞
some（一些）		複數名詞 ＋ 複數動詞
plenty（很多）		
a lot（很多）		
lots（很多）		
⋮		

UNIT 17～20

【比較】 Most *of my friends* **are** good students.

（我大部分的朋友都是好學生。）

4. *A number of* students *are* absent today.

$$\left\{\begin{array}{l} \text{a number of} + \textbf{複數名詞} \rightarrow \textbf{用複數動詞} \\ \text{the number of} + \textbf{複數名詞} \rightarrow \textbf{用單數動詞} \end{array}\right.$$

> a number of 的意思，一般字典上沒寫清楚，看下面的比較。
>
> one<a couple of<a few<several<a number of<many
> 一個　　二、三個　　　幾個　　幾個　　　好幾個　　　許多

a number of 好幾個（= *more than a few, but not many*）；
一些（= *some*）【詳見「麥克米倫高級英漢雙解詞典」p.1353】

【比較】 The number *of students* *is* supposed to be 20.

（學生人數應該是 20 人。）

5. There *is* a man and a woman at the door.

There is 和 There are，is 或 are 視後面主詞而定，但是有二個以上的主詞時，**動詞以靠近的主詞單複數為準**。【詳見「文法寶典」p.397】

6. Every man, woman, and child here *is* happy.

有二個以上主詞時，前面有 *each, every, many a, no*… 等修飾時，用**單數動詞**。【詳見「文法寶典」p.399】

Each boy and girl here *has* received a present.
（這裡的每個男孩和女孩都得到了一個禮物。）
No sound or voice *is* heard.（一點聲音都聽不到。）

7. Neither the students nor the teacher *wants* the party
to be cancelled.

A or B	
Either A or B	動詞與靠近者一致（不確定重點）
Neither A nor B	（敘述句與 B 一致，疑問句
Not only A but also B	與 A 一致）

這句話因為 teacher 是單數，所以動詞用 wants。【詳見
「文法寶典」p.399～p.400】
Are you or he to blame?（是你或他該受責備呢？）

8. Not you but I *am* in charge.
　　　主　詞

如果主詞是由肯定和否定組合而成時，動詞與肯定主詞一
致。句中對等連接詞 Not…but… 連接二個主詞，動詞
am 和肯定主詞 I 一致，因為重點在 I。
這句話也可說成：I, not you, am in charge.（是我，不是
你，負責。）　　*be in charge* 負責

9. Any *of your friends are* welcome to join us.

any 當主詞，**用單複數動詞皆可**，any 當形容詞時，可修
飾單數或複數名詞。【詳見「文法寶典」p.402, 171】
這句話也可說成：Any of your friends *is* welcome to
join us.，但現代英語有用複數動詞的傾向。

TEST *18* 主詞與動詞的一致

選出一個最正確的答案。

( ) 1. Each boy and each girl _____ to look nice.
    (A) wants   (B) want
    (C) are wanting   (D) have

( ) 2. Ten thousand dollars _____ a large sum of money.
    (A) is   (B) are
    (C) have been   (D) were

( ) 3. Whether I go or stay _____ on the news we get about Mother's health.
    (A) depends   (B) depending
    (C) dependent   (D) depend

( ) 4. The goods you ordered _____ arrived.
    (A) has   (B) have   (C) are   (D) is

( ) 5. There _____ sixty minutes in an hour.
    (A) are   (B) is
    (C) were   (D) shall be

( ) 6. Neither you nor I _____ happy.
    (A) are   (B) am   (C) is   (D) be

(   ) 7. _____ is right in this matter.
  (A) Both you and he
  (B) You as well as he
  (C) Not only you but also he
  (D) Both of you

(   ) 8. A poet and a musician _____ invited to dinner last night.
  (A) is   (B) are
  (C) was   (D) were

(   ) 9. All work and no play _____ Jack a dull boy.
  (A) make   (B) makes
  (C) be   (D) to

(   ) 10. Fire and water _____ not agree.
  (A) does   (B) do
  (C) is   (D) are

(   ) 11. Early to bed and early to rise _____ a man healthy, wealthy and wise.
  (A) make   (B) makes
  (C) made   (D) have made

(   ) 12. A number of students _____ part-time jobs.
  (A) has   (B) have
  (C) is   (D) are

UNIT 17 ~ 20

(　　) 13. Three-fourths of the earth's surface ＿＿＿＿＿
water.

    (A) is   (B) are

    (C) has been   (D) had

(　　) 14. Ham and eggs ＿＿＿＿＿ the main dish here.

    (A) is   (B) are   (C) be   (D) am

(　　) 15. Mathematics ＿＿＿＿＿ a difficult subject.

    (A) is   (B) are   (C) was   (D) were

【Answers】

1. **A** *Each boy and each girl* 意義上雖然是複數，但**動詞用單數**，因為說話者說到 each，every 或 no 時，自然用單數。【詳見「文法寶典」p.399】

2. **A** *Ten thousand dollars* (一萬元) 雖然是複數，但是表示「一個數目」，動詞用單數。凡是主詞為「一段時間」、「一筆金錢」、「一段距離」、「一個重量」時，形式為複數，但意義上為單數。【詳見「文法寶典」p.394】

3. **A** <u>*Whether I go or stay*</u> <u>depends</u> on the news *we get about*
　　　　名 詞 子 句

Mother's health.

我是否會去還是留在這，要視媽媽的健康情況而定。

Whether 引導名詞子句，做 depends on 的主詞，名詞子句當主詞，動詞用單數。

4. **B**　*goods*（商品）、*stairs*（樓梯）、*sweets*（糖果）等，常用
複數形。【詳見「文法寶典」p.84】

5. **A**　sixty minutes（六十分鐘）是複數，不是強調「一段時間」，
所以用複數動詞。

6. **B**

A *or* B
Either A *or* B
Neither A *nor* B
Not only A *but also* B

} 動詞與靠近者一致

7. **C**　理由同上。　(A) 和 (D) 須用複數動詞。

(C) You *as well as he are* right in this matter.

「你和他一樣」，重點在「你」，所以用 are。

A +

{
with
together with
as well as
but
except
}

+ B + **動詞**（動詞與 A 一致）

因為重點是強調 A。【詳見「文法寶典」p.400】

8. **D**　主詞是複數，動詞用複數，有 last night，用過去式。

【比較】*a poet and a musician*　一位詩人和一位音樂家

a poet and musician　一位詩人兼音樂家

【詳見「文法寶典」p.398】

9. **B**　【諺】只工作不遊樂，會使人變得遲鈍。

All work and no play（只工作不遊樂）是一件事，動詞用
單數。【詳見「文法寶典」p.399】　　dull〔dʌl〕*adj.* 遲鈍的

10. **B** 水火不相容。

兩個不同的單數名詞，用 and 連接，動詞用複數。

agree〔ə'gri〕v. 一致；和睦相處

11. **B** 【諺】早睡早起使人健康、有錢，又聰明。

Early to bed and early to rise（早睡早起）是一件事，用單數動詞。【詳見「文法寶典」p.399】

12. **B** 好幾個學生有兼職工作。　　*a number of* ①好幾個　②幾個

主詞是複數，動詞用複數。

13. **A** 地球表面有四分之三是水。

all
most
half
part
some　　+ of +　複數名詞→用複數動詞
a lot　　　　　　單數名詞→用單數動詞
lots
幾分之幾　　　【詳見「文法寶典」p.394】

one-fourth 四分之一

three-fourths 四分之三【分子大於一，分母要加 s】

14. **A** 火腿蛋是這裡的主菜。

ham and eggs（火腿蛋）是一道菜，用單數動詞。

【詳見「文法寶典」p.398】

15. **A** 有些學科名詞有 s，但意義上是單數，如：

mathematics（數學）、*physics*（物理學）、*politics*（政治學）、*economics*（經濟學）、*phonetics*（語音學）、*statistics*（統計學）等。【詳見「文法寶典」p.393】

UNIT *19*

五種基本句型
(Five Sentence Patterns)

● ●

英文以動詞爲核心，原則上，一個句子只有一個主要動詞，依動詞的性質分成五種基本句型。現在，

五種句型可歸納成一種句型：

> 主詞＋動詞（＋受詞/補語）
> S ＋ V（＋O / C）

有的動詞只適合一個句型，有的動詞適合多種句型，如 make 這個字，就適合五種基本句型。

 下面的劇情是你和外國朋友說你要去做衣服：

1.

I saw you leave.

I made for the tailor.

2.

He made me a new suit.

That's cool.

3.

It made me very happy.

I'll bet it did.

That's cool. 很酷。　　I'll bet it did. 當然。

= I'm sure it did. = That's for sure.

It looks great on you! 你穿起來很好看！
Great advice! 好建議！

19. 五種基本句型
（Five Sentence Patterns）

I *made* for the tailor. 　我去了裁縫店。

He *made* me a new suit. 　他給我做了一套新西裝。

It *made* me very happy. 　這件事使我眞高興。

【背誦技巧：三句都用 made】

I will *make* a handsome person. 　我會成為很帥的人。

Clothes *make* the man. 　【諺】人要衣裝。

A new look *made* all the difference. 　新的外表一切都改善了。

【前二句用 make，二、三句相關連】

This suit *was made* for me. 　這件西裝是爲我量身打造的。

I'm glad I *made* the decision. 　我很高興我做了這個決定。

The choice is yours to *make*. 　你也可以做這樣的選擇。

【第一句承接上段，二、三句相關連】

【文法解析】

1. I *made* for the *tailor*.　　　　　　　　　　S + V
   ‖　　　　　裁縫店
   left　　　= tailor's shop

   句中 made 是「完全不及物動詞」，和 left 意義相同。for the tailor 是介詞片語，當副詞片語用，修飾 made。

   也可把 ***made for*** 當成動詞片語，作「前往」解。

   I <u>made</u> <u>for</u> <u>the tailor</u>.　　　　　　　S + V + O
   主詞 動詞片語　　受　詞

   = I left for the tailor.

   make for　前往
   = ***leave for***
   = ***head for***

   凡是不需要受詞，也不需要補語的動詞，稱作「**完全不及物動詞**」。如：We all ***breathe***, ***drink***, and ***eat***.（我們都會呼吸、喝水，和吃東西。）breathe, drink 和 eat 在這個句子中是「完全不及物動詞」。再如：The moon ***rose***.（月亮升起了。）rose 在這個句子中，也是「完全不及物動詞」。「**完全不及物動詞**」有無限多，同樣一個動詞，有時及物，有時不及物，像 make 就可用在各種句型中。

2. He *made* me a new suit.　　　S + V + IO + DO
   給…做 間接　直接受詞
   　　　受詞

   made 作「給…做」解時，有兩個受詞，me 是間接受詞，a new suit 是直接受詞，這種動詞稱作「**授與動詞**」，類似的有：give（給）、lend（借）、bring（帶來）、show

（給…看）、tell（告訴）、write（寫信給）、send（送）、hand（拿給）、teach（教）、offer（提供）、sell（賣）、buy（買）、leave（留給）、do（= *give*）（給）、choose（選擇）、ask（問）等，**這類的動詞無限多，只要句意上有兩個受詞的動詞都可以。**【詳見「文法寶典」p.278】

3. It *made* me *very* happy.　　　S + V + O + OC
　　　　使　受詞　受詞補語

有些動詞接受詞後，還要接「補語」，才能使句意完全，這種接了受詞，句意還不完全的，稱作「**不完全及物動詞**」。
其他常須接受詞補語的動詞有：
① **感官動詞：** feel（感覺）、hear（聽到）、look at（看著）、listen to（聽）、notice（注意到）、observe（看到）、perceive（察覺到）、see（看到）、smell（聞起來）等。
② **使役動詞：** have（使）、let（讓）、make（使）、bid（叫）等。
③ **其他：** appoint（指定）、believe（相信）、call（叫）、choose（選擇）、command（命令）、consider（認為）等。【詳見「文法寶典」p.15】

4. I will *make* a handsome person.　　S + V + C
　　　　∥　　　　　　主詞補語
　　become

這種不接受詞，但須接補語對主詞加以補充說明的，稱作「**不完全不及物動詞**」。
① 其他常須接主詞補語的動詞有：
　　be 動詞、seem（似乎）、appear（看起來）、look（看起來）、sound（聽起來）、taste（嚐起來）、smell（聞起來）、

feel（感覺起來）、become（變成）、prove（結果是）、
turn out（結果是）、get（變得）、grow（變得）、turn
（變得）、remain（仍然是）、continue（持續）等。

② **常須接主詞補語的被動式動詞有：**

be made（被塑造成）、be thought（被認為）、be called
（被稱為）、be chosen（被選為）、be elected（被選為）、
be named（被命名為）、be appointed（被指派為）等，
這些動詞原來是「**不完全及物動詞**」，改成被動後，原
來的受詞變成主詞，受詞補語變成主詞補語。

例：We <u>elected</u> him <u>President</u>.   S + V + O + OC
       不完全及物動詞   受詞補語
（我們選他為總統。）

= He <u>was elected</u> <u>President</u>.   S + V + SC
   不完全不及物動詞片語   主詞補語
（他被選為總統。）

5. Clothes *make* the man.   S + V + O
         製造   受詞

make 當及物動詞，作「製造」解，如：

She ***made*** coffee *for all of us*.（她為我們大家煮咖啡。）
這種不需要補語的動詞，稱作「**完全及物動詞**」。

6. A new <u>look</u> *made* all the <u>difference</u>.   S + V + O
     核心主詞   核心受詞
     完全主詞   完全受詞

make all the difference 情況大有改善，make 是完全及物
動詞。

7. This suit *was made for me.*   S + V

任何及物動詞的被動，就是完全不及物動詞。

The tailor ***made*** me this suit.

= The tailor ***made*** this suit *for me.*

    完全及物動詞

（那位裁縫師為我做了這套西裝。）

【間接受詞和直接受詞對調，須加介詞】

= This suit ***was made*** *for me.*（這套西裝是為我而做的。）

    完全不及物動詞

8. I'm glad I <u>*made* the decision.</u>【make 是完全及物動詞】

       名詞子句

名詞子句做省略介詞的受詞。如果介詞不省略，就要寫成：
I'm glad for the fact ***that*** *I made the decision.*，that 子句
通常不能做介詞的受詞，加上 the fact，純粹為了滿足文法
上的需要，這句話文法對，但是美國人通常不說，因為太
囉嗦。有時又可以說，如：I'm glad for the fact that no
one saw me fall down.（我很高興沒有人看到我跌倒。）
何時說何時不說誰知道？只有背句子最安全。

9. The choice is yours *to make.*

在這裡，make 是「完全及物動詞」，不定詞片語 to make
修飾 yours，被修飾的 yours 是它意義上的受詞，不得再
加文法上的受詞 it，不可說成：*This choice is yours to
make it.*（誤）

TEST *19* 五種基本句型

選出一個<u>最正確</u>的答案。

( ) 1. How much does the smartphone _____?
    (A) take   (B) cost   (C) spend (D) use

( ) 2. The worker _____ only two hours repairing the machine.
    (A) took   (B) spent   (C) cost   (D) cast

( ) 3. Your suggestion seems to me very _____.
    (A) reasonable   (B) reasonably
    (C) reason   (D) not reason

( ) 4. I'm hungry now. Please _____.
    (A) give me a book
    (B) open the door
    (C) bring me some bread
    (D) call the police

( ) 5. When you are tired, you will feel _____.
    (A) sleepy   (B) sleep
    (C) sleeping   (D) sleeper

( ) 6. I would like to _____ that book from you.
    (A) lend   (B) lending
    (C) borrow   (D) borrowing

(　) 7. The cake smells _____.

  (A) good   (B) goodness

  (C) well   (D) sweetly

(　) 8. This material _____ like wool.

  (A) is felt   (B) feels

  (C) is feeling   (D) feel

(　) 9. This sweater looks _____ to the one I

  bought last night.

  (A) similar   (B) the same

  (C) alike   (D) different

(　) 10. His story sounds _____.

  (A) terribly (B) terror (C) terrify (D) terrible

(　) 11. A: What did your sister say?

  B: She _____ me a question.

  (A) asked   (B) explained

  (C) helped   (D) said

(　) 12. May I _____ your phone?

  (A) use   (B) borrow from

  (C) lend   (D) speak

(　) 13. What do you _____ this flower?

  (A) call (B) say (C) speak (D) tell

( ) 14. Father will buy a watch _____ me.
  (A) to   (B) for
  (C) by   (D) at

( ) 15. Please _____.
  (A) help me English
  (B) help me with my English
  (C) help me my English
  (D) help my English for me

【Answers】

1. B 「非人」做主詞，表示「花費」用 *cost*。
smartphone〔ˌsmɑrtˈfon〕*n.* 智慧型手機

2. B 人「花費時間」，用 *spend*。

3. A Your suggestion *seems* to me very reasonable.
     不完全不及物   主詞補語
seem 後應接形容詞，做主詞補語。
reasonable〔ˈriznəbl̩〕*adj.* 合理的

4. C 依句意，應選 (C) bring me some bread。
       間受 直接受詞

5. A 當你疲倦時，你會覺得想睡覺。
feel + 形容詞
sleepy〔ˈslipɪ〕*adj.* 想睡的

6. **C** *would like to* + 原形動詞　想要 (= *want to* + *V.*)

> lend + 間接受詞 + 直接受詞
> borrow + 直接受詞

7. **A**　smell（聞起來）
taste（嚐起來）
look（看起來）
feel（摸起來；感覺）
sound（聽起來）
　+ 形容詞（做主詞補語）

8. **B**　這個質料摸起來像羊毛。

feel like + **名詞**　感覺像；摸起來像
material〔 məˈtɪrɪəl 〕 *n.* 材料；質料　　wool〔 wʊl 〕 *n.* 羊毛

9. **A**　This sweater looks *similar* to the one *I bought last night*.
這件毛衣看起來和我昨天晚上買的很像。

be
look
　similar to　和⋯相似

(B) the same 後須接 as
(C) 句子應改成：These two sweaters *look alike*.
(D) different 後須接 from

10. **D**　sound + 形容詞

11. **A**　She <u>asked</u> <u>me</u> <u>a question</u>.
　　　　　授與動詞 間受　直接受詞
其他選項須加 to，但句意還是不合理。

12. **A** 向別人借電話可用 use 或 borrow，lend 需要二個受詞，borrow 是及物動詞。

13. **A** What do you call this flower? 你怎麼稱呼這種花？

疑問代名詞 ***What*** 引導疑問句，在句中，做 call 的**間接受詞或受詞補語**。

14. **B** 授與動詞的**間接受詞**和**直接受詞**的位置對調，**須加介系詞**。

Father will buy me a watch.
間受　直接受詞

= Father will buy a watch *for me*.
副詞片語

直接受詞和間接受詞之間，

① **介詞用 for 的有**：buy, make, leave, choose, order, sing, do 等。

② **介詞用 to 的有**：give, lend, bring, show, tell, write, send, hand, teach, offer, sell, promise, pass 等。

③ **介詞用 of 的有**：ask。【詳見「文法寶典」p.278】

15. **B** 有些動詞，在間接受詞和直接受詞之間要有 ***with***，如：help（幫助）、supply（供給）、provide（提供）、serve（供應）等。【詳見「文法寶典」p.280】

Please help me with my English.
間受　　　　直接受詞

這句話的意思是「請幫助我學英文。」只能幫助人，不能幫助事物，所以不能說：*Please help my English.*（誤）

UNIT *20*

相關詞構句（Correlative）

· ·

英文有些語詞成雙成對地出現，如：one…the other（一個…另一個），one…the others（一個…其餘的），one thing…(and) another（一回事…另一回事），這種句子稱作「相關詞構句」。在會話中，或寫文章時，使用相關詞，會使你的表達比較生動。

 這一回你是主角，你和你的外國朋友談到你的家人。

That's noble of you.　你很高尚；你很了不起。
noble〔'nobḷ〕*adj.* 高尚的

Trust your instincts. 相信你的直覺。

It's a fascinating city. 這個都市很迷人。

20. 相關詞構句（Correlative）

I have three brothers; *one* is in the States, and *the others* are here.

Either they *or* I am responsible for the family.

It is true my mother is old, *but* she is healthy.

【背誦技巧：這是一篇故事】

我有三個兄弟；一個在美國，其他的在這裡。

不是他們，就是我，要為這個家庭負責任。

我的母親確實是老了，但是她很健康。

She is *not only* knowledgeable *but also* interesting.

Some say this, *others* say that, but I don't care.

To say is *one thing*, to do is *another*.

【第一句承接上段，二、三句都有 say】

她不僅有學問，而且又風趣。

有人這樣說，有人那樣說，但我不在乎。

說是一回事，做又是另一回事。

I live in Taipei *not because* I love the city, *but because* I am paid well.

Here we can enjoy *both* Chinese culture *and* modern society.

It is *neither* too hot *nor* too cold.

【三句都談論台北市】

我住在台北，不是因為我愛這個城市，而是因為薪水高。【幽默】

在這裡我們可以享有中國文化和現代社會。

天氣既不會太熱，也不會太冷。

【文法解析】

1. I have three brothers; *one* is in the States, and *the others* are here.

   有兩個的時候，用 *one*…and *the other*（一個…另一個），有三個或三個以上，用 *one*…and *the others*（一個…其餘的）。

   【比較】I have three brothers; *one* is in the States, *another* is in Japan, and *the other* is here.

   （我有三個兄弟；一個在美國，另一個在日本，還有一個在這裡。）【詳見「文法寶典」p.141】

   I have two brothers; *one* is in the States, and *the other* is here.（我有兩個兄弟；一個在美國，另一個在這裡。）　　*the States* 美國（= *the United States*）

2. *Either* they *or* I am responsible for the family.

   either…or（不是…就是）是表「選擇」的連接詞，連接兩個主詞時，動詞和第二個主詞一致。

   be responsible for 對～負責

3. *It is true* my mother is old, *but* she is healthy.
   = *To be sure*, my mother is old, *but* she is healthy.
   = *Indeed*, my mother is old, *but* she is healthy.

   It is true (*that*)…, *but*
   To be sure, …, *but*　　（的確…但是）【表「讓步」的強調語氣，
   Indeed, …, *but*　　　　　　詳見「文法寶典」p.471】

   It is true 後面的 *that* 可以省略或保留。【詳見「麥克米倫高級英漢雙解詞典」p.2143】

4. She is *not only* knowledgeable *but also* interesting.

   對等連接詞 *not only*…*but also*（不僅…而且）連接兩個形容詞。

   knowledgeable〔'nɑlɪdʒəbl〕 *adj.* 有學問的
   interesting〔'ɪntrɪstɪŋ〕 *adj.* 有趣的

5. *Some* say this, *others* say that, but I don't care.

$$\begin{cases} \text{some···others} & \text{有些···有些} \\ = \text{some···some} \end{cases}$$

這句話也可説成：*Some* say this, ***and*** $\begin{Bmatrix} some \\ others \end{Bmatrix}$ say that,

but I don't care. 一般都省略 and。中國人思想是「有些···有些···」，美國人可説 "*Some...some...*" 或 "*Some...others...*"。再次證明，學英文背句子最安全。

6. To say is *one thing*, to do is *another*.

one thing···another　一回事···另一回事

這句話也可説成：To say is *one thing*, ***but*** to do is *another*. 句中的 but 可以省略。

7. I live in Taipei *not because I love the city, but because I am paid well.*

not because···but because（不是因爲···而是因爲）連接兩個表「原因」的副詞子句，修飾 live。【詳見「文法寶典」p.512】

pay〔pe〕*v.* 付薪水

8. *Here* we can enjoy *both* Chinese culture *and* modern society.
　　　　　　　　　　　名詞片語
　　　名詞片語

對等連接詞 ***both···and*** 連接兩個名詞片語，做 enjoy 的受詞。

9. It is *neither too* hot *nor too* cold.

對等連接詞 ***neither···nor***（既不···也不）連接兩個形容詞。
【詳見「文法寶典」p.468】

中國人習慣説「不冷也不熱」，美國人卻習慣把 hot 放在前面。
It is neither too cold nor too hot.【文法對，但不合乎美國人習慣】

TEST *20* 相關詞構句

選出一個<u>最正確</u>的答案。

(   ) 1. One of my sisters lives in the States, and
              _____ are here with us.
    (A) others   (B) the others
    (C) the other   (D) another

(   ) 2. To learn is one thing; to teach is _____.
    (A) the other   (B) another
    (C) others   (D) other

(   ) 3. It is true he is old, _____ he is still strong.
【詳見「文法寶典」p.180, 289】
    (A) and   (B) that   (C) but   (D) for

(   ) 4. He has two brothers. One is in the U.S. and
              _____ is in China.
    (A) another   (B) the other
    (C) other   (D) one

(   ) 5. Not only wealth _____ also health is
important.
    (A) but   (B) and   (C) or   (D) that

(   ) 6. This is not imagination, _____ reality.
    (A) and   (B) or   (C) also   (D) but

(　) 7. One of his parents will come with him; _____
will stay home.
    (A) another　　　　(B) the others
    (C) the other　　　　(D) the one

(　) 8. This book is _____ interesting and
instructive.
    (A) both　(B) either　(C) neither　(D) but

(　) 9. _____ men sow, so will they reap.
    (A) If　　(B) Until　　(C) Unless　　(D) As

(　) 10. Some students have classes on Saturdays;
_____.
    (A) so do all students　(B) the boy is absent
    (C) others don't　　　　(D) but I have, too

(　) 11. _____ are interesting, the others aren't.
    (A) All stories　　　(B) Some of the stories
    (C) Some the stories　(D) Some of stories

(　) 12. I don't like John. I don't like Peter. I like
_____.
    (A) nobody
    (B) John and Peter
    (C) either John or Peter
    (D) neither John nor Peter

UNIT 17 ~ 20

( ) 13. Things will change, _____ you like it or not.

【詳見「文法寶典」p.180, 287】

(A) that　(B) which　(C) whether　(D) but

( ) 14. _____ overwork and what with undernourishment, he fell ill. 【詳見「文法寶典」p.469】

(A) What by　　(B) What with
(C) Because　　(D) What if

( ) 15. It is not that I am unwilling _____ I have no time. 【詳見「文法寶典」p.512】

(A) not because　　(B) because
(C) but that　　(D) but

【Answers】

1. **B** *one…the others* 一個…其餘的 (= *one…the rest*)

2. **B** 學是一回事，教又是另一回事。
   …is one thing…is another …是一回事，…又是另一回事

3. **C** *It is true~, but…* 的確~，但是…
   = Indeed~, but…
   = To be sure~, but…

4. **B** 兩者中的「另一個」，用 *the other*。

5. **A** 「*not only…but also*」(不僅…而且) 連接兩個主詞，*also* 可以省略。

6. **D** *not* A *but* B 不是 A，而是 B　這不是想像，而是事實。

7. **C** 父母親中的「另一個」，用 *the other*。

8. A 「*both…and*」連接兩個形容詞。

這本書既有趣，又有教育性。

This book is $\left\{\begin{array}{l} \textbf{\textit{both}} \\ \textbf{\textit{at once}} \\ \textbf{\textit{equally}} \end{array}\right\}$ interesting *and* instructive.

instructive〔ɪnˈstrʌktɪv〕*adj.* 有教育性的

9. D *As men sow*, so will they reap.

According as　also

這句話要從後面開始翻譯，so will they reap 是主要子句。

「人將收成什麼，按照他所種的而定。」引申為「種瓜得瓜，

種豆得豆。」【詳見「文法寶典」p.502】

10. C *some…others* 有些～有些

11. B some of *the* stories (這些故事中有一些)，範圍有限定，

所以，剩餘的故事要用 *the others* (= *the rest*)。

12. D 「兩者都不」喜歡，用 *neither…nor*。

13. C Things will change, *whether you like it or not*.

（ 無論你喜不喜歡，事情都會改變。）

whether 引導副詞子句，修飾 change，此時 or not 不可

省略。whether 引導名詞子句時，or not 可省略。

14. B *What with overwork and (what with) undernourishment*,

he fell ill.

（ 一方面由於工作過度，一方面由於營養不良，他就生病了。）

what with…, and (what with) … 半因…半因…【表原因】

【詳見「文法寶典」p.469】

15. C *not that…but that…* 不是因為…而是因為…

= *not because…but because…*【詳見「文法寶典」p.512】

不是因為我不願意，而是因為我沒有時間。

UNIT 17～20

UNIT 21~24

UNIT *21*

冠 詞（Articles）

• •

冠詞 a, an 和 the，屬於形容詞。原則上，普通名詞要加冠詞，物質名詞、抽象名詞、專有名詞不加冠詞，但例外很多，背句子是最簡單的方法。

 這一回是你和外國朋友談到你的運動方式。

21. 冠 詞 (Articles)

Exercising gives us *energy*.	運動使我們有活力。
I don't *play basketball* very often.	我不常打籃球。
Walking to *school* is a kind of exercise.	走路上學是一種運動。

【背誦技巧：三句話都和運動有關】

I don't eat *breakfast* at home.	我不在家吃早餐。
I *grab a bite* here and there.	我四處找東西吃。
I don't take *the MRT* or *the bus*.	我不搭捷運或公車。

【一、二句和吃東西有關】

The campus is not too far from my place.	校園離我家不太遠。
I enjoy passing by *Dr. Sun Yat-sen Memorial Hall*.	我喜歡經過國父紀念館。
I like to see people practice *martial arts* there.	我喜歡看人們在那裡練武功。

【說明走路上學的經過】

【文法解析】

1. Exercising gives us *energy*.

   energy〔'ɛnədʒɪ〕*n.* 活力 是抽象名詞，不加冠詞。原則上，抽象名詞、物質名詞、專有名詞不可數，也不加冠詞。這句話也可說成：Exercise gives us energy.

2. I don't *play basketball* very often.

   原則上，普通名詞要加冠詞，但是**運動、遊戲的名詞前不加 the**。

   【例】Do you play *bridge*?（你玩橋牌嗎？）

3. Walking to *school* is a kind of exercise.

   school（學校）、college（學院）、church（教堂）、market（市場）、bed（床），指建築物本身或場所時，是普通名詞，要加冠詞；**指用途時，為抽象名詞，不加冠詞**。

   【比較】I go to <u>school</u> every day.（我每天**上學**。）
   　　　　　　　　抽象名詞
   　　　　I live near *the* <u>school</u>.（我住在學校附近。）
   　　　　　　　　　　　　普通名詞

4. I don't eat *breakfast* at home.

   原則上，普通名詞前要有不定冠詞 a 或 an，但 breakfast（早餐）、lunch（午餐）、dinner（大餐）、supper（晚餐）前，不加冠詞。

5. I *grab a bite* here and there.

   grab〔græb〕*v.* 抓　　bite〔baɪt〕*n.* 一口（食物）
   grab a bite 吃東西【詳見「一口氣背會話」p.55】
   here and there 四處；到處

以下是有 a 的慣用語：

as a rule（照例地；通常）、as a whole（整體看來）、all of
a sudden（突然間）、be at a loss（茫然不知所措）、in a
hurry（匆忙地）、at a distance（隔遠一些）。

【例】I *am* quite *at a loss* what to do.（我茫然不知所措。）
The picture looks better *at a distance*.
（這幅畫隔遠一些看較好。）

6. I don't take *the MRT* or *the bus*.

原則上，專有名詞不加冠詞，但**捷運、鐵路、政府機關
等，前面須加 the**，如 the MRT（捷運）、the High
Speed Rail（高鐵）、the Ministry of Education（教育部）。
句中 bus 是普通名詞，須加 the，take the bus（搭公車），
如果改成：I don't go to school by bus.（我不搭公車上
學。）by + 交通工具，就不加 the。【詳見「文法寶典」p.219】

7. *The campus* is not too far from my place.

campus〔'kæmpəs〕*n.* 校園 是普通名詞，須加冠詞，這
裡的 campus 指的是「學校」，美國人常用 campus 代替
school。　　*my place* 我家（= *my home*）

8. I enjoy passing by *Dr. Sun Yat-sen Memorial Hall*.

專有名詞不加冠詞，類似的有：Chiang Kai-shek Memorial
Hall（中正紀念堂）、Taipei 101（台北 101 大樓）、228 Park
（228 公園）、Daan Forest Park（大安森林公園），但「總統府」
the Presidential Building 就要加 the，因為是政府機關。

9. I like to see people practice *martial arts* there.
martial〔'marʃəl〕*adj.* 戰爭的；戰鬥的
ˌ*martial* '*art*　（東方）武術（如功夫、空手道、柔道等）
普通名詞的複數，不加冠詞。

TEST *21* 冠　詞

選出一個最正確的答案。

(　　) 1. My dream is to go to _____ Sun Moon
Lake and _____ Mt. Ali.
(A) the ; the　　　　　(B) a ; a
(C) X ; X　　　　　　(D) a ; the

(　　) 2. I read _____ China Post every day.
(A) the　　(B) x　　(C) a　　(D) an

(　　) 3. How about coming for _____?
(A) the dinner　　　　(B) our dinner
(C) dinner　　　　　　(D) a dinner

(　　) 4. I decided to go to _____ United States.
(A) the　　(B) x　　(C) a　　(D) an

(　　) 5. He was elected _____.
(A) a chairman　　　　(B) the chairman
(C) his chairman　　　(D) chairman

(　　) 6. What kind of _____ do you like best?
(A) a book　　　　　　(B) book
(C) the book　　　　　(D) the books

(　　) 7. There is _____ university around here.
(A) the　　(B) an　　(C) a　　(D) x

(　) 8. You had better buy _____ umbrella with UV protection.
　　　(A) the　　　(B) an　　　(C) a　　　(D) x

(　) 9. They delivered the fliers _____.
　　　(A) from one door to the other
　　　(B) from door to door
　　　(C) from the door to the door
　　　(D) from a door to a door

(　) 10. She was _____ soon after she got married.
　　　(A) with child　　　　(B) with a child
　　　(C) with her child　　(D) with one child

(　) 11. She looks more beautiful _____.
　　　(A) in the distance　　(B) at a distance
　　　(C) in a distance　　　(D) at the distance

(　) 12. I love him _____ because he is honest.
　　　(A) the more　　　　(B) all the more
　　　(C) all more　　　　(D) not more

(　) 13. He likes to play _____.
　　　(A) basketball　　　(B) a basketball
　　　(C) the basketball　　(D) basketballs

(　) 14. The massage is charged _____.
　　　(A) by hour　　　　(B) by an hour
　　　(C) by the hour　　　(D) by hours

(　) 15. He waited, _____.
　　　　(A) with hat in his hand　　(B) hat in his hand
　　　　(C) with a hat in hand　　(D) hat in hand

【Answers】

1. **C** 專有名詞原則上都不加冠詞。

2. **A** 書籍、雜誌、報紙等專有名詞，須加定冠詞 *the*。
　　the China Post 英文中國郵報

3. **C** 普通名詞原本須加冠詞，但三餐名詞 *breakfast*, *lunch*, *dinner*, *supper* 是例外，不加冠詞。

4. **A** 複數形（字尾有 s）的專有名詞要加 *the*，如 *the United Nations*（聯合國）。【詳見「文法寶典」p.63】

5. **D** 當補語，表示官職、身分、頭銜的名詞，不加冠詞。
　　【詳見「文法寶典」p.221】
　　elect〔ɪˋlɛkt〕*v.* 選舉　　chairman〔ˋtʃɛrmən〕*n.* 主席

6. **B** *a kind of*, *a sort of*, *a type of* 後的單數普通名詞不加冠詞。【詳見「文法寶典」p.223】

7. **C** university〔͵junəˋvɝsətɪ〕*n.* 大學，雖然第一個字母 u 是母音，但第一個發音 /j/ 是子音，故用 *a university*。

8. **B** umbrella〔ʌmˋbrɛlə〕*n.* 傘，第一個字母 u 讀成 /ʌ/ 是母音，故用 *an umbrella*。
　　你最好買一把防紫外線的傘。　　*UV* 紫外線（= *ultraviolet*）

9. **B** 兩個相對名詞不加冠詞,如 ***from door to door*** (挨家挨
戶),***father and son*** (父子),***day and night*** (日夜)。
【詳見「文法寶典」p.222】
deliver 〔 dɪ'lɪvɚ 〕 *v.* 遞送　　flier 〔'flaɪɚ 〕 *n.* 傳單

10. **A** 她結婚後很快就懷孕了。

$$\begin{cases} \textbf{\textit{with child}} \ \ 懷孕 \\ \text{with a child} \ \ 帶著孩子 \end{cases}$$ 【詳見「文法寶典」p.224】

11. **B** 她遠一點看比較漂亮。

$$\begin{cases} \textbf{\textit{at a distance}} \ \ 遠一點 \\ \textbf{\textit{in the distance}} \ \ 在遠處 \end{cases}$$

12. **B** $\begin{cases} \textbf{\textit{all the}} + 比較級 \ \ 更~【all the 是加強比較級的語氣】 \\ \textbf{\textit{all the more}} \ \ 更加 \\ \textbf{\textit{all the better}} \ \ 更好 \end{cases}$
因為他很誠實,我更加喜歡他。

13. **A** 運動、遊戲的名詞前不加 the。

14. **C** 按摩以小時收費。
表示單位的名詞前要加 ***the***。【詳見「文法寶典」p.219】
charge 〔 tʃɑrdʒ 〕 *v.* 收費;控告;充電

15. **D** He waited, *hat in hand*.

= He waited, *with a hat in his hand*.
表狀態的副詞片語,常省略介系詞和冠詞。
stick in hand 手上拿著拐杖 (= *with a stick in his hand*)
cap in hand 手上拿著帽子 (= *with a cap in his hand*)

UNIT 22

句尾附加句（Attached Sentence）

. . . .

　　「句尾附加句」就是一個簡單形式的省略句。
凡是一句話講完後，要對前面的話加以補充，以加
強或說明，就要用到「句尾附加句」。學口語學到能
用「句尾附加句」很難，用背句子的方法最簡單。

 下面你是主角，這些是和你的另一半
為小孩的功課吵架時所說的話。

22. 句尾附加句
（Attached Sentence）

I'm sorry—*I really am*.	我很抱歉，我真的很抱歉。
I love you—*I really do*.	我愛你，我真的愛你。
I don't think you are happy, *are you*?	我覺得你不快樂，對不對？

【背誦技巧：一、二句成對出現】

You don't want to do it, *and neither do I*.	你不想做，我也不想做。
Let's talk, *shall we*?	我們談一談，好嗎？
Let's not fight, *all right*?	我們不要吵架，好嗎？

【二、三句成對出現】

He must have failed, *didn't he*?	他一定是失敗了，對不對？
We should help him, *shouldn't we?*	我們應該幫助他，對不對？
I believe he is the best student, *isn't he*?	我相信他是最好的學生，對不對？

【談論到另一個人】

【文法解析】

1. I'm sorry—*I really am*.

   這句話要當作慣用句來看，I really am. 是句尾附加句。
   美國人常說：I'm sorry. I'm sorry from the bottom of
   my heart. ***I really am.***（我很抱歉。我打從心底感到抱歉。
   我真的很抱歉。）此時就是三個句子。
   破折號用於加強語氣。【詳見「文法寶典」p.42】

2. I love you—*I really do*.

   這句話要當作慣用句來看，I really do. 是句尾附加句。
   Michael Jackson 在演唱會時，常說："I love you.
   I love you from the bottom of my heart. ***I really do.***"
   （我愛你們。我由衷地愛你們。我真的很愛你們。）

3. I don't think you are happy, *are you*?

   「句尾附加句」有個簡單的方法解決，句子的主要思想
   （不一定是主要子句）是否定的，後面用肯定。在這裡的
   are you? 是 ***are you happy***? 的省略。【詳見「文法寶典」p.7】

4. You don't want to do it, *and neither do I*.

   neither do I 是 neither do I want to do it 的省略。這句
   話也可變成兩句：You don't want to do it. Neither do I.

5. Let's talk, *shall we*?

   Let's 引導的肯定命令句用 ***shall we***? 表「提議」，在這裡
   是 ***shall we talk***? 的省略。

6. Let's not fight, *all right*?

Let's 引導的否定命令句，「句尾附加句」用 *all right*? 或
O.K.?。【詳見「文法寶典」p.6】也可説成：Let's not quarrel,
all right? (我們不要吵架，好嗎？)

fight〔faɪt〕*v.* 打架；吵架　　quarrel〔'kwɔrəl〕*v.* 吵架

7. He must have failed, *didn't he*?

「must have + p.p.」表現在推測過去，*didn't he*? 是
didn't he fail? 的省略。這句話可加長為：He must
have failed *in the exam*, didn't he? (他一定考試沒考好，
對不對？)

【比較】He *must have been* a fool, *wasn't he*?
(他一定是個笨蛋，對不對？)
【wasn't he 是 wasn't he a fool 的省略】

8. We should help him, *shouldn't we*?

前面肯定，後面用否定，*shouldn't we* 是 *shouldn't
we help him* 的省略。

9. I believe he is the best student, *isn't he*?

主要思想是「他是最好的學生」，前面肯定，後面用否定，
isn't he? 是 *isn't he the best student*? 的省略。你不能
説：*I believe he is the best student, don't I*? (誤)，因為
句意不合理，你不可能説成：*...don't I believe so*? (誤)

TEST *22* 句尾附加句

選出一個<u>最</u>正確的答案。

(　　) 1. This is the first time you've seen this movie, _____?
    (A) hadn't this   (B) haven't I
    (C) is it   (D) isn't it

(　　) 2. He _____ to New York by train, didn't he?
    (A) goes   (B) has gone
    (C) went   (D) have gone

(　　) 3. Mary broke the window, _____?
    (A) didn't she   (B) didn't Mary
    (C) did she   (D) did not she

(　　) 4. Paul called on his teacher, _____?
    (A) was he   (B) wasn't he
    (C) did he   (D) didn't he

(　　) 5. Do it yourself, _____?
    (A) will you   (B) don't you
    (C) do you   (D) doesn't it

(　　) 6. Stand up, _____?
    (A) don't you   (B) will you
    (C) aren't you   (D) are you

(　　) 7. Mary read that magazine, _____?
    (A) does she   (B) doesn't she
    (C) did she   (D) didn't she

( ) 8. Yesterday Jennifer stayed home all day, _____?
      (A) don't she   (B) didn't she
      (C) doesn't she   (D) wasn't she

( ) 9. There is nothing worth seeing, _____?
      (A) isn't there   (B) isn't it
      (C) is there   (D) is it

( ) 10. He's never been there, _____?
      (A) is he   (B) wasn't he
      (C) has he   (D) hasn't he

( ) 11. It feels good, _____?
      (A) isn't it   (B) don't it
      (C) doesn't it   (D) wasn't it

( ) 12. My sister has to come here, _____?
      (A) hasn't she   (B) doesn't she
      (C) has she   (D) does she

( ) 13. Let's go there, _____?
      (A) shan't we   (B) shall we
      (C) don't we   (D) aren't we

( ) 14. You did promise to help me, _____?
      (A) didn't you   (B) did you
      (C) were you not   (D) were you

( ) 15. We couldn't get a table near the window,
      _____ we?
      (A) could (B) can (C) did (D) were

【Answers】

1. **D** 前面肯定，後面用否定，前面是 is，後面用 isn't。

2. **C** went 配合後面的 didn't。

3. **A** *didn't she* 是 *didn't she* break the window 的省略。

4. **D** *didn't he* 是 *didn't he* call on his teacher 的省略。

5. **A** 命令句的句尾附加句用 *will you*，表「請求」，*will you* 是 *will you* do it yourself 的省略。

6. **B** *will you* 是 *will you* stand up 的省略。

7. **D** *didn't she?* = *didn't she* read that magazine?

8. **B** *didn't she?* = *didn't she* stay home all day? 句尾附加句就是簡單型式的疑問句。

9. **C** 前面是 *There is* nothing，句尾附加句用 *is there*，是 *is there* anything... 的省略。

10. **C** *has he?* = *has he* been there?

11. **C** 感覺很好，對不對？ *doesn't it* 是 *doesn't it* feel good 的省略。

12. **B** *doesn't she* 是 *doesn't she* have to come here 的省略。

13. **B** Let's 後面的句尾附加句，用 *shall we* 表「提議」， *shall we* 是 *shall we* go 的省略。

14. **A** *didn't you* 是 *didn't you* promise to help me 的省略。

15. **A** 前面用 We couldn't，後面用 *could we*？

UNIT *23*

介系詞（Preposition）

介系詞又稱「前置詞」，因為放在名詞前面。介系詞省略後，原來的名詞變成副詞，常常讓人困惑。有時介系詞後面又接了介系詞片語，讓人更頭痛。如果知道「介系詞＋介系詞」又稱「雙重介系詞」，就容易多了。背完這一回九句，解決你所有的疑惑。

 下面是你和你的朋友講手機的內容。

23. 介系詞 (Preposition)

Where *the heck* are you?	你到底在哪裡？
I arrived *around four*.	我四點左右就到了。
I have waited *an hour*.	我已經等了一個小時。

【背誦技巧：等很久，打電話找人】

It's already *past* five.	已經過了五點了。
What time will you be here?	你何時會到這裡？
The restaurant is *opposite* McDonald's.	餐廳在麥當勞對面。

【一、二句指時間】

The door is *dark red*.	門是暗紅色的。
The waiter is *busy serving* other diners.	服務生正忙著服務其他的客人。
We can't order *till after* he's finished.	我們要等到他服務完別人才能點菜。

【二、三句都在說服務生】

【文法解析】

1. Where *the heck* are you?

   the heck 究竟；到底 (= *the hell*)

   the heck 前省略了介系詞 in。這句話也可説成：

   Where *in the heck* are you? (你究竟在哪裡？)，但較少用。

   【比較】 Where *the heck* are you?【語氣委婉，男女皆可用】

   　　　　 Where *the hell* are you?【語氣粗魯，只有男生用】

   　　　　　　　　【詳見「一口氣背會話」p.1262】

2. I arrived *around four.*

   中文説：「我四點鐘左右已經到了。」英文卻不能説成：

   I have arrived around four. (誤)，因爲過去的時間要用

   過去式。【詳見「文法寶典」p.336】

   這句話省略了介系詞 **at**。也可説成：I arrived **at** around

   four.

3. I have waited *an hour.*

   an hour 前面省略了 *for*。這句話也可説成：

   I have waited *for an hour.* 時間名詞前的介系詞可省略。

   凡是表示**時間、距離、重量、價值、次數、程度、狀態**等

   名詞前的介系詞常省略。【詳見「文法寶典」p.100 , p.546】

4. It's already *past* five.

past（過了）是過去分詞轉變成的介系詞。【詳見「文法寶典」
p.544 , 598】

5. *What time* will you be here?

疑問形容詞 What 加上 time 引導疑問句，**在時間名詞
前省略了 At**。這句話也可説成：*At* what time will
you be here? 但較少用。

6. The restaurant is *opposite* McDonald's.

near（接近）、**opposite**（在…對面）**等後面的 to 常省略**，
它們是由形容詞轉變而來的介系詞。【詳見「文法寶典」
p.544 , 546】這句話也可説成：The restaurant is opposite
to McDonald's.

7. The door is *dark red*.

「of + 形容詞 + 名詞」做補語時，of 常省略。
這句話也可説成：The door is *of* dark red. 但較少用。

8. The waiter is *busy serving* other diners.

busy（忙碌的）、**occupied**（忙碌的）、**employed**（從事
於）、**engaged**（從事於）**等形容詞後的介系詞 in 常省
略**。這句話不可説成：*The waiter is busy in serving
other diners.*（誤）
diner〔ˈdaɪnɚ〕*n.* 用餐者；吃飯的客人

9. We can't order *till after he's finished.*

order〔ˋɔrdɚ〕*v.* 點餐

finished〔ˋfɪnɪʃt〕*adj.* 做完的；完成的

介詞片語主要是當形容詞片語或副詞片語用，有時為了句意需要，會當名詞片語，做介系詞的受詞，這種情況不多，是文法家硬歸納的，**背句子是最簡單的方法**。在這個句子中，after 子句竟然做 till 的受詞。

當兩個介系詞在一起，稱為「**雙重介系詞**」，有：**from among**、**from behind**、**from under**、**till after**、**in between** 等。【詳見「文法寶典」p.544, 545】**till after** 後面接子句和名詞均可。

例： Please stay *till after dinner.*

（請留到晚餐以後。）

I took the paper *from under the desk.*

（我從書桌底下拿出那張紙。）

I heard a noise *from behind the curtain.*

（我聽到從窗簾後面傳來的聲音。）

TEST *23* 介系詞

選出一個<u>最正確</u>的答案。

(　) 1. We usually stay at home ＿＿＿＿ Christmas.
(A) in　　(B) into　　(C) to　　(D) for

(　) 2. Please wait a while; I will come ＿＿＿＿ a minute.
(A) of　　(B) on　　(C) in　　(D) by

(　) 3. Why was she angry ＿＿＿＿ herself?
(A) for　　(B) to　　(C) with　　(D) about

(　) 4. Hard work will result ＿＿＿＿ success.
(A) in　　(B) to　　(C) from　　(D) for

(　) 5. He bought the house ＿＿＿＿ a low cost.
(A) with　　(B) in　　(C) on　　(D) at

(　) 6. I think I have to thank her ＿＿＿＿ person for the wonderful birthday gift she gave me.
(A) with　　(B) by　　(C) in　　(D) of

(　) 7. Don't do things ＿＿＿＿ your will.
(A) to　　(B) against　　(C) by　　(D) with

(　) 8. Though he is young, he can see ＿＿＿＿ a difficult problem.
(A) in　　(B) into　　(C) to　　(D) for

(   ) 9. I have no hobbies _____ playing tennis.
       (A) without   (B) beside
       (C) expect   (D) except

(   ) 10. John is sweet _____ the girl next door.
       (A) on   (B) off   (C) for   (D) of

(   ) 11. Within hours, help will be _____ the way.
       (A) in   (B) into   (C) at   (D) on

(   ) 12. The police informed the prisoner _____ his legal rights.
       (A) with   (B) for
       (C) of   (D) against

(   ) 13. Mary's ability is always superior _____ Debbie's.
       (A) in   (B) than   (C) of   (D) to

(   ) 14. Please don't make faces _____ me.
       (A) at   (B) on   (C) with   (D) for

(   ) 15. We must keep them _____ getting to know our plans.
       (A) of   (B) for   (C) from   (D) in

【Answers】

1. **D**　*for* + 名詞表「**目的**」，for Christmas「爲了聖誕節」，
   on Christmas Day「在聖誕節當天」。

2. **C**　*in* a minute　再過一分鐘；再過一會 ⎫　*in* 用於未來式，
   in an hour　再過一小時 ⎭　表「**再過**」。
   【詳見「文法寶典」p.614】

3. **C**　⎧ *be angry with* + 人
   ⎩ *be angry about* + 事

4. **A**　⎧ *result in*　導致
   ⎩ *result from*　起因於

5. **D**　*at* a low cost　以低價 ⎫　*at* 表「以~價格；以~代價」
   at a good price　以好的價錢 ⎭　【詳見「文法寶典」p.557】

6. **C**　*in person*　當面；親自 (= *face to face*)

7. **B**　*against* one's will　違反某人的意願 ⎫　*against* 做「違反；
   against the law　違法 ⎭　反對」解
   【詳見「文法寶典」p.550】

8. **B**　*see into*　了解；調查，在此做「了解」解，等於 understand。

9. **D**　*except* 做「除了~之外」解。【詳見「文法寶典」p.570】

10. **A**　*be sweet on*　愛上；迷戀
    = *be in love with*
    = *be very fond of*

11. **D** ***on the way*** 在途中
   on the market 出售中 ⎫
   on the alert 警戒中 ⎭ ***on*** 表「在～狀態中」

12. **C** 警方告知犯人他的法律權利。

inform（通知）	warn（警告）
accuse（控告）	rob（搶）
cheat（欺騙）	remind（提醒）
cure（治療）	relieve（減輕）

＋人＋ of ＋事、物

【詳見「文法寶典」p.279】

13. **D** ***be superior to*** 優於【詳見「文法寶典」p.203】
   be inferior to 劣於

14. **A** ***make faces at*** 對～做鬼臉
   make eyes at 對～拋媚眼

15. **C** ***prevent***
   stop
   keep

   prohibit
   discourage ⎬ ***sb. from*** doing sth.
   deter 阻止某人做某事

   hinder
   restrain

UNIT 24

比 較（Comparison）

• •

　　一般人最搞不清楚的 **no more than**，**no less than**…等，詳細文法分析不如先背句子，會說以後再了解文法，便能舉一反三。如：no more～than「和…一樣不」，如果你背一個句子，You are no more rich than I.（你和我一樣沒錢。）你就不會忘記了。

這一回你是主角，談到借錢的問題，
這些比較級的慣用語你會說，你的
英文就更道地了。

1.
I have not more than one hundred dollars.
That's enough.

2.
I need not less than five hundred.
Not a problem.

3.
You are no more rich than I.
That's true.

24. 比 較（Comparison）

I have *not more than* one hundred dollars.	我最多有一百元。
I need *not less than* five hundred.	我需要至少五百元。
You are *no more* rich *than* I.	你和我一樣沒錢。

【背誦技巧：not more than–not less than–no more…than】

John has *no more than* one thousand dollars.	約翰只有一千元。
He can lend me *no less than* five hundred.	他能借我多達五百元。
He is *more than* helpful.	他不只是樂於助人。

【只有一千──最多借五百──非常樂於助人】

John is *more* kind *than* generous.	與其說約翰慷慨，不如說他仁慈。
He is *much* kind*er than* any other boy.	他比任何其他男孩都仁慈。
I like him *best*.	我最喜歡他。

【一、二句都強調 kind】

【文法解析】

1. I have *not more than* one hundred dollars.

   not more than 字面意思是「不超過」，引申為「最多」
   (= *at most*)。這句話可加長為：I have *not more than*
   one hundred dollars with me. (我身上最多一百元。)

2. I need *not less than* five hundred.

   not less than 字面意思是「不少於」，引申為「至少」(= *at least*)。這句話可說成：I need *at least* five hundred
   dollars.

3. You are *no more* rich *than* I.
   ‖
   not at all

   這句話字面意思是「你一點都沒有比我有錢。」，也就是「你
   和我一樣沒錢。」

   > 公式： no more ~ than
   >   = not ~ any more than   和…一樣不

   這句話可說成：

   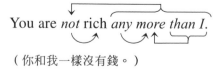

   You are *not* rich *any more than* I.

   (你和我一樣沒有錢。)

4. John has *no more than* one thousand dollars.

no more than 字面意思是「一點都不超過」，引申爲「只有」(= *only*)，no 在比較級形容詞前爲副詞，等於 not at all。

5. He can lend me *no less than* five hundred.

no less than 字面意思是「一點都不少於」，引申爲「多達」(= *as much as*)，強調很多。這句話也可說成：He can lend me *as much as* five hundred.

⎧ not more than　最多 (= *at most*)
⎩ not less than　至少 (= *at least*)

⎧ no more than　只有 (= *only*)
⎩ no less than　多達 (= *as much as*)

重點在片語中的 no，等於 not at all。
【詳見「文法寶典」p.202】

6. He is *more than* helpful.

more than 是成語，做「不只是；不止；非常」解，等於 not just 或 very，這句話也可說：He is *not just* helpful. (他不只是樂於助人。) 又如：I am *more than* grateful. (我非常感謝。)

7. John is *more* kind *than* generous.

這句話字面意思是「約翰的仁慈大過於慷慨」，引申爲「與其說約翰慷慨，不如說他仁慈。」

同一人兩種性質比較時，用 *more…than*。

He is *more* kind *than* generous. 【正】
He is kinder than generous. 【誤】

8. He is *much* kind*er than any other boy*.

使用比較級時，必須把自身除外，常與 other 或 else 連用。
原則上，very 修飾原級，much 修飾比較級。【詳見「文法寶典」p.207】

9. I like him *best*.

原則上，形容詞的最高級要加 the，副詞的最高級不加 the，
但是，後面有修飾語限定時，the 可加可不加，例如：

I like spring *best*. (我最喜歡春天。)
I like spring (*the*) *best* of all the seasons
of the year.
(一年的季節中，我最喜歡春天。)

of 引導的片語通常是形容詞片語，如 a man *of means* (有
錢人），但 the best 在這裡是副詞，文法上沒辦法解釋，可
能因為 the best 常當名詞用。先有語言，才有文法，所以
往往有例外，因為說話者已經習慣用 the best of…。【詳見
「文法寶典」p.262】

TEST *24* 比較

選出一個<u>最正確</u>的答案。

( ) 1. John came _____ than all the others.
    (A) later   (B) latest   (C) latter   (D) last

( ) 2. You are _____ student in the school.
    (A) the diligentest   (B) more diligent
    (C) diligenter   (D) the most diligent

( ) 3. _____ the players on our baseball team, Jim
    is the best.
    (A) Through   (B) Between
    (C) Among   (D) Around

( ) 4. This is _____ plan I have ever made.
    (A) bad   (B) worse
    (C) the worst   (D) the badest

( ) 5. As Edison grew _____, he never lost his
    interest in science.
    (A) elder   (B) more old
    (C) oldest   (D) older

( ) 6. The more you learn, the more _____ you
    can get a job.
    (A) easily   (B) easy
    (C) ease   (D) easiness

(   ) 7. He is the taller _____ the two boys.
     (A) than   (B) in
     (C) of   (D) between

(   ) 8. He has three times _____ books as I have.
     (A) as many   (B) more
     (C) many   (D) as much

(   ) 9. Every day our world becomes _____.
     (A) smaller and smaller
     (B) small and small
     (C) small and smaller
     (D) little and little

(   ) 10. People have to keep the environment as clean

     _____.
     (A) as possible   (B) as they are possible
     (C) as can possible (D) as can

(   ) 11. The pedestrian has _____ rules to follow as
     the driver of a vehicle.
     (A) as many   (B) so much
     (C) more   (D) such

(   ) 12. This is _____ than that.
     (A) much good   (B) very better
     (C) very good   (D) much better

( ) 13. A cow is _____ as a horse.
    (A) strong as an animal
    (B) as a strong animal
    (C) as strong an animal
    (D) as an animal strong

( ) 14. This material is _____ that.
    (A) the same thick as
    (B) the same thickness as
    (C) as thickness as
    (D) as same thick as

( ) 15. She dances more _____ than her elder sister.
    (A) beautiful   (B) beauty
    (C) beauties   (D) beautifully

【Answers】

1. **A** John came ***later** than all the others.*

late「晚」的比較級是 *later*。

2. **D** You are ***the most diligent** student in the school.*
diligent ('dɪlədʒənt) *adj.* 勤勉的，最高級是 the most
diligent。

3. **C** 在我們棒球隊員之中，吉姆是最棒的。

among 表「在～之中；其中之一」，與最高級連用。

【詳見「文法寶典」p.552】

4. **C** 這是我曾經做過最糟糕的計劃。

bad 的比較級是 *worse*，最高級是 *worst*。句中 *ever* 等於 *at any time*。

5. **D** 隨著愛迪生年齡逐漸增長，他從未失去對科學的興趣。

grow older 變老；長大 (= *get older*)

6. **A** *The more you learn*, *the more* easily you can get a job.
　　　　副詞子句

你學得越多，越容易找到工作。【詳見「文法寶典」p.504】

7. **C** *of the two* 代替 than，比較級前要加 the。

【詳見「文法寶典」p.201】

8. **A** He has *three times as many* books *as I have*.

他有的書是我的三倍。

倍數副詞放在第一個 *as* 前面。【詳見「文法寶典」p.182】

9. **A** 比較級 + *and* + 比較級 (越來越…)

smaller and smaller 越來越小

fatter and fatter 越來越胖

colder and colder 越來越冷

UNIT 21~24

10. **A** 人們必須保持環境儘量乾淨。

 as~as possible 儘可能~，源自 *as~as it is possible*。

11. **A** 行人要遵守的規則和汽車駕駛人一樣多。【as~as 爲原級比較】

 … has *as many* rules *to follow as the driver*….

 pedestrian〔pəˈdɛstrɪən〕*n.* 行人

12. **D** *very* 修飾原級，*much* 修飾比較級。【詳見「文法寶典」p.207】

13. **C** *so, as*
        } + 形容詞 + *a(n)* + 名詞【詳見「文法寶典」p.216】
 too, how

14. **B** 這種材料和那種一樣厚。

 the same…as（同樣的）【表種類、意義、數量、性質、程度等相同】
 the same…that（同一個）

 This is *the same* knife *as* I lost.

 （這把小刀和我遺失的那把一樣。）【不是同一把】

 This is *the same* knife *that* I lost.

 （這就是我遺失的那把小刀。）【同一把】

 【詳見「文法寶典」p.127, 200】

15. **D** She dances *more beautifully than* her elder sister.

 修飾動詞要用副詞。

歡迎參加「一口氣背文法」背誦比賽

　　自從發明了「一口氣背會話」後，我就想編一本有關文法的會話書，想了十幾年，才想到這種簡單的方法，編成了「一口氣背文法」，編劇情很困難，非常感謝和我一起工作20幾年的夥伴，蔡琇瑩老師和謝靜芳老師，我自己從沒想到能夠完成這本書，以後同學使用這本書，既可以學會話，也可學文法。

　　我們務求書中的每一句話，都可以脫口而出。我們要學的東西很多，學了用不到就是浪費，浪費時間就等於浪費生命。我過去浪費了很多時間學英語會話，曾經和外國老師在一起十幾年，每天拿錄音機不停地修正自己，但效果有限，發明「一口氣背會話」後，會話能力快速增強，每天有書背，不亦樂乎！

　　小孩子背了「一口氣英語」後，會說英語、會演講，媽媽高興得不得了，但是，他們一碰到學校考試就傻眼了，很多小時候從雙語幼稚園培養起來的孩子，上了國中，不得不回到升學補習班，做文法試題的訓練，從「口說英語」回歸「啞巴英語」，向傳統的英語教學法投降。

　　我們有一位天才兒童韓德妘，上了「一口氣英語班」，和外國老師對答如流，也可以用英語演講，她問我下面這條題目：

The moon _____ around the earth.
(A) move   (B) moves   (C) moving   (D) moved
答案：(B)

她說，moon是單數，為什麼用複數moves呢？所以，完全沒有學文法的小孩，碰到文法題目就不會做，她不曉得動詞時態有12種，她不曉得主詞第三人稱單數，動詞現在式要加s，就像許多美國人，會說英文，但寫出來的句子不一定對，「一口氣背文法」正好解決這個問題。

　　文法規則太多，學到連接詞忘了名詞，一輩子也學不完。「一口氣背文法」216句，每個句子代表一個文法規則，背完馬上可以用在日常生活當中。我們請專業美籍播音員錄音，每一個Unit是一軌（track），只要用手機掃描QR碼，九句話反覆地聽，不須專心，也自然能背下來。我們還要舉行「一口氣背文法」背誦比賽，優先背好前100名同學，可得獎學金2,000元，歡迎同學參加。

　　憑本書可至台北市許昌街17號6F「劉毅英文」，領取「一口氣背文法背誦手冊」，裡面附有比賽辦法詳細說明。

劉毅

全書 1～24 回

一口氣背文法
Learning Grammar
with One Breath English

附錄音 QR 碼　售價：280 元

主　　　編 / 劉　毅

發　行　所 / 學習出版有限公司　　　☎ (02) 2704-5525

郵 撥 帳 號 / 05127272 學習出版社帳戶

登　記　證 / 局版台業 2179 號

印　刷　所 / 裕強彩色印刷有限公司

台 北 門 市 / 台北市許昌街 10 號 2F　　☎ (02) 2331-4060

台灣總經銷 / 紅螞蟻圖書有限公司　　　☎ (02) 2795-3656

本公司網址　www.learnbook.com.tw

電 子 郵 件　learnbook@learnbook.com.tw

2019 年 10 月 1 日新修訂

4713269381129

背短句是學英語的秘訣。

背的句子說起來有信心。

每一個 track 有一個 Unit，
不停地聽，自然會背。

背完本書，再做完試題，
文法實力無人能比。